GW01606499

SCOTTISH SHORT STORIES

SCOTTISH SHORT STORIES 1976

Preface by Edwin Morgan

COLLINS
St James's Place London

William Collins Sons & Co Ltd
London · Glasgow · Sydney · Auckland
Toronto · Johannesburg

First published 1976

Published with the support of the Scottish Arts Council

ISBN 0 00 222462 3

Set in Linotype Pilgrim
Made and Printed in Great Britain by
William Collins Sons & Co Ltd Glasgow

CONTENTS

Preface by Edwin Morgan 7

Janet Caird
THE DEPRIVED 9

Alan Jackson
THE CONSPIRACY FOR ARTHUR 21

George Mackay Brown
THE FEAST AT PAPLAY 24

Robert Crampsey
BISHOP'S MOVE 46

Carl MacDougall
THE BLIND READING 65

William Grant
SPUD: SUFFERING THROUGH SUNDAY 68

Oswald Wynd
WHO WANTS THE TWENTIETH CENTURY ANYWAY? 97

P. M. Hubbard
THE PEN OF MY AUNT 110

Gordon McGill
SCOTCH HENRY 121

CONTENTS

Paul Mills

BREAD 133

Graham Petrie

THE INTERVIEW 145

Giles Gordon

NINETEEN POLICEMEN SEARCHING THE SOLENT SHORE 158

Kirkpatrick Dobie

HIGH AND LIFTED UP 179

Naomi Mitchison

CALL ME 187

Arthur Young

THE CLOWN AS LOVER 197

Anne Turner

A LASTING IMPRESSION 206

Biographical Notes 217

PREFACE

QUANTITATIVELY, the short story seems to be a flourishing form in Scotland, if the large number of submissions for the present volume is anything to go by. If the short story, as is sometimes said, has fallen on evil days, the obvious enthusiasm of response from so many writers would seem to leave jeremiahs without a leg to stand on. In this sense, it is clear that the double initiative of the Scottish Arts Council and Messrs Collins has proved useful and productive and has every justification.

Qualitatively, it is rather like the waters of Loch Lomond – there is a steep descent. My fellow-editors (Philip Ziegler and Trevor Royle) would I think concur with me in finding a distressing preponderance of the backward look. Reminiscence, nostalgia, kailyard melodrama filled many pages. Even when stories did deal with contemporary life, a veil of stereotyped attitudes and expressions too often kept reality at bay. Freshness and accuracy, surprisingness without slickness – these virtues of the short story need to be more strenuously cultivated. The masters of the form – Chekhov, Maupassant, Babel – are able to suggest, by the careful placing of a few telling details, the atmosphere and weight, the wrongness or the longing, of a whole society. Scottish writers could learn much from them. Scotland, after all, is becoming an increasingly interesting place to live in. Must cognizance of this be so muffled, so gingerly, so grudging? What Jack London, or Gorky, would not do with oil and the north-east!

But enough. What we have, we have. I hope the stories in this collection will show something of the range and competence of the work that is being done; the variety of approach, of setting, and of style, is pleasant to discover, and distinctly encouraging. If editors are permitted their exhortations, they must also in fairness give honour where honour is due. We trust readers of these stories will find much to interest them, and will be well disposed towards this annual series. Outlets for short stories are far from numerous, even when radio is added to magazines and newspapers, and a yearly roundup does at least give some accessibility and permanence to the best examples. We were unable, for reasons of space, to include everything we would have liked to put in, and this may be an argument for further thinking on how short stories might be published and collected. But in the meantime we recommend this volume as a going concern.

E.M.

THE DEPRIVED

JANET CAIRD

I REMEMBER the very first time I saw The Roses thinking what a wonderful exercise in camouflage it was. On that beautiful June day with the sun blazing, and the famous rose-beds in their first outburst of bloom, it looked wonderful.

The long low house with its old grey sandstone walls covered with Gloire de Dijon roses was charming, and the extensions had been skilfully added at the back so as not to spoil the effect when one emerged from the shady drive into the open ground before the house. The entrance hall prolonged the effect; low-ceilinged, with a wide shallow beautiful wooden staircase leading from it. Everywhere gleaming wood, beautiful rugs, and a huge silver rose-bowl filled with flowers reflected in an antique mahogany table. If it wasn't a fine old country house, it must be a very good hotel: and even though one knew it wasn't, it was a shock when the crisp white uniform of a nurse appeared to ask your business. I got used to the set-up, of course, but the first impression was always at the back of my mind through all the long months when I visited my Aunt Sophia there.

Aunt Sophia was the last member of my mother's family. With the exception of a brother drowned at sea, they had all lived well into their eighties. My mother had reached eighty-nine. Aunt Sophia was ninety-two. She, alone of the family, was extremely wealthy, having been left what seemed to the rest of the family a vast fortune by a doting husband. She was childless and had been a wonderful aunt to all her nieces and nephews. When at last it became clear that she must have skilled nursing, and it being impossible to find private help, it was only natural that she should move into The Roses: The Roses being, in the geriatric world, the equivalent of Claridge's or the Savoy in the normal world. I don't know what the fees were at The Roses, all that being handled by Sophia's lawyers, but they were certainly vast.

Not that the inmates didn't get value for money. They did. The furnishings, food, nursing were all of the highest standard. Everywhere the emphasis was on immaculate freshness, cleanliness, perfection. The roses in the flower-vases always seemed newly-picked. I never saw a fallen petal or a faded flower all the time I visited there. It was the acme of discreet good taste. No effort, no detail, was spared to veil the reality of the slow drifting from life of the patients.

And this was more than an elaborate exercise in public relations. When I came down from Aunt Sophia's room on that first day, I was met by a discreet and charming secretary who asked me to call in at Dr Mactaggart-Thom's office. Dr Mactaggart-Thom was medical director and part-owner of The Roses. I must admit that I went in with some prejudice. He would, I was sure, be large, smooth, smell of expensive after-shave and have soft white hands. Not at all. Dr Mactaggart-Thom was certainly tall but very lean, brown (he was a keen fisherman and commuted to Scotland whenever possible), with a firm grasp and a faint tang of snuff. It was all rather reassuring after the smooth perfection outside his office. Dr Mactaggart-Thom was, among other things, an astute business man. He was also, and with absolute sincerity, passionately interested in and concerned about his patients.

He greeted me courteously, motioned me to a chair and said:

'I always like to have a little chat with our guests' nearest relatives. I understand you are in the position of being Mrs Hope's next-of-kin.'

'Yes, I am.'

'I like to explain just what the principle is on which we run The Roses, so that friends and relations can play their part in the therapeutic arrangements.'

'"Therapeutic"?' I said. 'I should have thought any curative procedures were not on . . .'

'Ah, there you are mistaken, Mrs Grant. Some of our guests *do* go back home. But I agree, for the majority, that is not possible. So our aim must be to keep them happy. You may have noticed that we do our best to make their surroundings here as far removed from a hospital atmosphere as possible . . .'

I made affirmatory noises.

'But we go further. We never, I repeat never, mention the possibility of – ah – their final departure. Our nurses are instructed never to hint at such a thing, or even discuss it among themselves. And we earnestly ask relatives and friends to do the same.'

'You mean,' I said, 'that we must never use the word -----.'

He raised a hand.

'Please. It is never uttered in here. Except perhaps by a guest who has newly arrived. But they soon stop using it, and indeed, I am convinced, even thinking of it, surrounded as they are by so many of the pleasant things of life. And if they ever do show signs of – ah – restiveness, we calm them down.'

'With drugs?'

'Various ways and means. A little hypnotic treatment, a glass of good wine . . . The thing is, they are kept cheerful, happy, and do not think of the future . . . We protect them from it.'

He paused. I was silent, thinking of my mother's last illness and the year she had spent in the local geriatric hospital, a place supplied with all the necessities and none of the luxuries; a place of humour and sadness and steady indestructible human courage, where, as my mother had remarked casually one day, 'the wings are always hovering' and no one had any illusions about the outcome . . .

'You don't approve?' Dr Mactaggart-Thom had a penetrating eye. I had been silent too long.

'I shouldn't dream,' I said, 'of in any way interfering with the principles on which you run The Roses. I'll co-operate to the best of my ability.'

'Thank you, Mrs Grant. I was sure you would understand.'

I could certainly undertake to co-operate: but I couldn't answer for Aunt Sophia, who was a strong-minded woman and still remarkably alert mentally. But to my surprise she slipped into the atmosphere of The Roses from the start. The day was skilfully broken up by mealtimes, elevenses and so on. There were cosy little sessions of physiotherapy and occupational therapy – if patients wanted to weave bags, embroider tapestry, they could. Aunt Sophia declined. 'I've always hated sewing and I won't begin now.' There was a library of light novels, which she read with relish. And a small colour TV by each bed provided some contact with the outside world. The TVs surprised me. Meeting Dr Mactaggart-Thom one day as he admired a splendid bed of roses, I said:

'Doesn't the TV distress the patients? I mean the violence and sudden -----.'

He raised a deprecating hand.

'Please, not that word. And "guests" rather than "patients". Hmm? No. TV does not disturb them. To them, it is something quite outside them and not quite real . . . and it fills the day. The great thing is to avoid blank spaces; otherwise they may begin to have unpleasant thoughts. Ah! Here's the car. Excuse me. One of our guests is going back home – a proud moment for us. He was quite convinced that he – that life held nothing more for him when he came. Now he is returning home.'

From beside the rose-bed I watched while an old man, walking with a tripod, was packed into a large and shiny car and driven off beside an anxious-faced middle-aged woman. Then I made my way to Sophia's room. Perhaps what I had just seen did justify all the luxury, the cocooning against reality. Perhaps ignoring the facts could be therapeutic. That afternoon I saw Sister.

'Is there any likelihood that Mrs Hope will ever be able to go home? I saw a p—, a guest leaving today.'

Sister shook her head.

'Not a chance. And Mr Penhurst will be back in a month. They all come back.'

I had to admit to myself that Sophia was as happy – if one could use the word about a totally negative absence of unpleasantness – as was possible for a person in her condition. She lived, apparently, from moment to moment, never thinking of the future but lingering among the pleasanter memories of the past. She rapidly built up a strong attachment to her room-mate (there were no single rooms at The Roses; they encouraged 'undesirable introspection', I was told). I never knew Miss Shivas's first name; following the convention of their time they were always 'Mrs Hope' and 'Miss Shivas' to each other. She was perhaps not as mentally alert as Sophia – at times she seemed to slip into another time-stream – but physically she was in better shape, did quite a lot of physiotherapy, and could make her way up and down the corridor with the help of a zimmer. She also, I gathered, had a niece who visited her at intervals but our paths never crossed. Aunt Sophia and she seemed to spend a lot of time exchanging reminiscences; occasionally, to their vast content, finding they had common acquaintances at some remote connection. Altogether, I began to feel that Sophia was probably in as satisfactory circumstances as the situation allowed.

Time passed. The rose-beds declined into winter austerity – not shabby, as my roses always looked in winter; it was clear these roses enjoyed every advantage, and were being tended with all the horticultural skill available, to mitigate the disadvantages imposed by the routine of nature. Christmas was celebrated at The Roses with exactly the right note of good taste – a beautiful Christmas tree, holly and evergreens, a suitable present for each guest. Sophia got an amazing number of cards; Miss Shivas very few; I sent her one myself. I learnt with surprise that she was even older than Sophia and must have had few friends left. Her niece sent a magnificent bouquet of out-of-season flowers, which, to my amusement, rather roused the envy of Sophia, who ordered me to send her a similar display at her own expense.

On the other hand, Easter went by unnoticed; not surprisingly, it being difficult to celebrate Easter if you've put a taboo on Good Friday.

One day at the end of May, when I went into Sophia's room, she was not in her bed. Miss Shivas told me she was having her hair done – a hairdresser came regularly to the little hairdressing-room at the end of the corridor – and would be back soon. I sat down to wait and made conversation.

'You're fortunate here in having a hairdresser coming.'

'Yes indeed. We are very well looked after.' She raised her head from the heaped-up pillows. 'Not only all this – ' waving a thin hand latticed with the prominent veins of old age round the room – 'but in other ways.'

She beckoned me to lean closer.

'Before I came here, I was afraid, *very* afraid. But not any more.' Her voice, surprisingly clear for one of her age, dropped; her glance shifted sideways, and she said, softly and clearly but not addressing me:

'It happened to the others, but it won't to me, no, never, never to me.'

I had seen her have one of these lapses, when it was as if a cog missed and her mental grip on things slipped, and I was going to take her hand and draw her back to reality when Sophia was wheeled in, splendidly blue-rinsed and very cheerful. Sister followed behind; she gave a sharp glance at Miss Shivas, nodded to me and said brightly:

'Miss Shivas! Time for your walk,' and at once the cog slipped back and the old lady was herself again.

A fortnight later, when I came to see Sophia before going off on holiday, Miss Shivas was progressing down the corridor with two tripods, helped by a physiotherapist and watched by Sister. I paused to watch too.

'Will Miss Shivas be going home soon?' I asked.

Sister looked startled.

'"Going home"?'

'She seems so much more active.'

'Oh, I see. Well, there are problems.'

'I suppose it depends on her niece.'

'Well, yes, it does rather. And relatives aren't always willing . . .'

Aunt Sophia was in an unusually morose mood, due entirely to the fact that I was going away for a fortnight.

'Shan't have any visitors,' she said. 'I've got used to you coming in.'

'Oh but you will have visitors,' I said, and mentioned a few names. 'Besides, you've got your television to look at.'

'I never do look at it. All the plays are full of fighting and nasty things. Just put it on and you'll see.'

I switched on. It was a news bulletin and the little screen was filled with soldiers with guns at the ready running down a street towards a column of smoke billowing up with slow menace. In the foreground two ambulance men knelt by a woman lying in an ominous sprawl.

'You see,' said Sophia petulantly, 'that's what I mean. Always something nasty. They shouldn't put on plays like that.'

'It isn't a play.' But I said no more, switched off, and talked of other things. As I went out into the sunlight I thought that Dr Mactaggart-Thom would probably be highly delighted with Miss Shivas and Aunt Sophia. The one didn't believe it would happen to her and the other didn't believe it happened to other people. It might be highly satisfactory to the good doctor, but for myself . . . But I was off on a fortnight's holiday and I was firmly resolved to put The Roses and all it implied behind me.

When I entered Aunt Sophia's room on my first visit after returning, Miss Shivas's bed was empty. After greeting Sophia and handing over the small present I had brought, I said:

'Where's Miss Shivas?'

'She's gone home.'

'"Gone home"?'

At first I wondered, but Sophia went on:

'Yes, her niece came for her. Quite suddenly, and we didn't get a chance to say goodbye. They had wheeled me into the sun balcony, and when I came back she was gone. But I've had a letter from her. There it is. You can read it.'

A sheet of notepaper lay on her locker. I lifted it. It was a grey-blue colour, oddly stiff and with a faint musty smell as if it had been kept for a long time in a damp cupboard. The writing was faint and spidery but legible enough, and the contents were brief. Miss Shivas was sorry she hadn't had time to say goodbye and was missing their nice talks.

'It was nice of her to write,' I said.

'Yes it was, and when I feel like it, I'll answer.'

Miss Shivas's bed remained unoccupied. I made unobtrusive enquiries and Sister said they found it harder to fill beds owing to having to put charges up. Aunt Sophia certainly seemed to miss the company and I began to see a deterioration in her condition; she was less alert, less cheerful. So I was quite glad when after about a week she greeted me with more animation than she'd shown for some time and said:

'I've had another letter from Miss Shivas. There it is.'

I took the letter from the envelope. The paper still smelt damp and musty; the writing was even frailer. It was a sad little letter. Miss Shivas didn't feel at home; she had nothing in common with the other people, looked back with regret on her pleasant conversations with Mrs Hope, and would like to think they could meet again. She remained hers affectionately.

'She doesn't seem very happy,' I said, as I put the letter back into the envelope. For a moment I wondered what was odd about it.

'The letter isn't stamped, Aunt Sophia. How did it get here?'

'How do I know?' She was unusually querulous. 'It was there when I woke up. I expect her niece handed it in.'

'Probably. I see she uses the same notepaper as you do. but it must have been in a cupboard for a long time.'

'What does it matter? I'm tired. I think you'd better go.'

It was then I realized how quickly she was failing. Three days later I got word that she had passed away.

All the arrangements were, of course, made with the utmost tact. When everything was over, I paid a last visit to The Roses to pick up her personal effects. When I arrived there was no one about; the whole place was quite silent with an early-afternoon hush. The guests were all asleep, all lapped in a vast make-believe, carefully cocooned against the last experience available to them . . . I went up to Sophia's room. The two beds were made up, immaculate; the room a model of airy freshness. Sophia's travelling clock, her silver-backed brushes, her writing case were neatly arranged on her locker. And on top of the writing case, an envelope.

Yes. Another letter from Miss Shivas; unstamped. Her niece couldn't have heard . . .

I forced myself to open it. The mustiness was even more marked; it was almost an earthy smell: the writing was fainter, in places illegible, but one phrase stood out:

'I feel quite lost here.'

Some little sound made me look up. Sister stood in the doorway.

'Oh, good afternoon, Sister. There was no one about, so I just came up.'

'That's all right. I think everything is in order.'

'Yes indeed. And I'd like to thank you for all the care my aunt enjoyed.'

'Well, it's our job, you know. We try to make our guests happy.'

'I know. Poor Miss Shivas doesn't seem too happy, now she's gone.'

'Miss Shivas?'

I hadn't realized before that Sister must be much older than she appeared. And why was she so white?

'She's written two or three times to my aunt, but they're rather sad letters.'

'But she can't have.'

'But she has. Here's a letter I found today.'

I held it out to her. The earthy smell lingered between us. Sister backed against the locker, her hands raised in rejection.

'She can't have. Miss Shivas is dead; she died when you were away. She's dead; dead and buried.'

The forbidden words hung in the air and into their aftermath came a sharp order.

'Sister, you had better go to my office.'

Dr Mactaggart-Thom stood aside to let her pass. Then he turned to me. 'I'm sorry about that. Sister forgot herself – perhaps she has been doing too much.'

I was bundling Sophia's things into the case and didn't answer.

'I am sorry,' he repeated.

I looked at him. All I could see were the bones of his

skull sharp beneath the skin and the rigid rictus of his smile. I brushed past him and ran down the stairs, through the gleaming silent hall, past the rose-beds, down the drive and back into my world of life and death.

THE CONSPIRACY FOR ARTHUR

ALAN JACKSON

ONCE UPON a time there was a conspiracy. It was a conspiracy for Arthur. Began this way.

About half past nine on a Friday night, in the Spotted Dick, Colin saw this willowy and billowing, thrilling and dare-devilling, darkhaired whitefleshed longdressed whish of a chick.

She was really a person called Moira. But Colin was young, drunk, a man, with friends – he saw a chick.

She saw a chin, a moustache, nice lips, fond hot honest humorous eyes watching and letching.

She stayed watching his eyes and he stood witching hers, so she, not to move too quick and give the game, raised her little drinking glass and smiled behind it, knowing the smile would not look definite, would leave him doubtful, but that, if there *was* anything in this, 'twould be enough.

He waited, she waited. He cracked jokes with mates, she said to girl-friend: 'No, not yet. Might as well wait a minute or two.'

Bogwards bound Colin casually to both of them (only slightly lingering on Moira):

'Fancy coming to a party?'

Friend looked at Moira – oh just a light glimmer. Moira nodded back – oh just a tot.

'Yeah, all right. Why not?' says friend.

Is there any hope for us? Any hope for Arthur? Why not straight to Moira did the cleanbrowed Colin go saying:

You are so fantastic I
've just got to ask you out.
Say no and you will slay me,
Please believe.

'S rarely done so well.

'S mostly done in a glancy, dead cool, modern, unromancy, self-protect, frightened to be wrecked, we'd only have necked, vile style.

But for wee Arthur, wondrous wee wet Arthur's sake, it worked.

Oh who was closer in a taxi that night than Colin and Moira as they began to chat, and, amongst others, gather the whereabouts of each other's flat?

She was a saucy typist but not daft. He was a thinking man, hence unemployed.

'Thought we were going to a party. Where drink?'

'What? Not smoked pot? Just as thought. You wait, remember the date, off by rote. For tonight, sweetpie, you fly, you float.'

He rymbled on. She, won by words' delicious flow, sat glowing warm, not melted quite, almo.

At the party (i.e. the pad arty – always enough people about to pretend there was something happening each week-end) Colin's prob. was to separate Moira off; find somewhere genial and venient where they could, if she would, was in the mood, start to doff.

His urgent though relaxed manœuvrings met with

success. In ten minutes they were out of the press:

'Let's go somewhere where's it's less . . .'
and they were in his little room,
'scuse mess.'

Sitting on the one clear space, the bed, they knew it. They sat and said nothing while he rolled a joint and she looked round it and they still knew. They caught each catching other looking and they knew it again. Were so suspended they could hardly smile but they did smile and when they both really knew both knew, she lay back on his arm as he put it round her and both were down. And as she looked his looking face came near.

Kissed. A long time. A long time to find and to lose a long time. Sometimes he opened his eyes and hers were shut and sometimes she opened her eyes and his were shut and sometimes one knew other's were open and stayed shut until all were open and nothing was shut. And they laughed at each other.

Almost a cry, although merry, inside such a laugh, and a shy, and a stir of fear, for whatever was happening was happening in time and by chance.

The conspiracy of Arthur has begun.

His eyes were blue and hers were brown and I feel no need to go on describing further down.

The eyes for the wise are the prize and nothing else that may open or rise should surprise.

Arthur's eyes are blue, his hair quite fair, considering the darkness of the pair. He's eighteen months, runs about, piddles and chatters.

Two have become one and that's what matters.

THE FEAST AT PAPLAY

GEORGE MACKAY BROWN

Thora, the mother of Earl Magnus, had invited both the Earls to a banquet in Holm after their meeting on Easter Monday, and Earl Hakon went there after the murder of the holy Earl Magnus. Thora herself served at the banquet, and brought the drink to the Earl and his men who had been present at the murder of her son. And when the drink began to have effect on the Earl, then went Thora before him and said, 'You came alone here, my lord, but I expected you both. Now, I hope you will gladden me in the sight of God and men. Be to me in stead of a son, and I shall be to you in stead of a mother. I stand greatly in need of your mercy now, and I pray you to permit me to bring my son to church. Hear this my supplication now, as you wish God to look upon you at the day of doom.'

The Earl became silent, and considered her case, as she prayed so meekly, and with tears, that her son might be brought to church. He looked upon her, and the tears fell, and he said, 'Bury your son where it please you.'

Then the Earl's body was brought to Hrossey, and buried at Christ's Kirk (in Birsay) which had been built by Earl Thorfinn.

– *The Orkneyinga Saga*

IN THE morning Sverr the fisherman came up from the shore to the Hall of Paplay and called in at the kitchen door, 'Hallo, there. I have this basket of haddocks.' Gudrun the housekeeper appeared. 'Hallo, Gudrun,' said Sverr. 'The Lord is risen. Here is the fish.'

'Don't take your sea-stink into the kitchen,' said Gudrun. 'Wait here at the door. The Lord is risen.'

Ingerth called from her loom, 'Who is there, Gudrun?'

'Sverr the fisherman,' said Gudrun. 'He has a basket of haddocks, lady. He wants paid for them now.'

'My mother-in-law is in the chapel,' said Ingerth. 'Tell the man he'll be paid after Mass.'

'I've a good mind to take the fish away,' said Sverr. 'Fishermen can't wait. We could easily sell them among the hill farms.'

'The lady Thora will pay you as soon as she comes in from the chapel,' said Gudrun. 'Just sit at the door for half an hour or so. It's Easter Monday – I hope you've been to the church yourself.'

'Some folk have to earn their living,' said Sverr sourly, and sat down on the stone at the door, beside his basket of fish.

'The Lord is risen,' said Gudrun happily. She went back to the kitchen and sat on the fireside stool. The floor about the stool was strewn with red and white and black feathers, and from a rafter three dead naked chickens hung by their claws. Gudrun picked up a fourth chicken and began to pluck it. Feathers swirled about her feet like snowflakes. She heard someone calling outside, 'Gudrun, Gudrun, I've come with the pig. Do you want him killed now?'

It was John the herdsman. He carried a young fat placid boar under his arm.

'Yes, kill it,' said Gudrun. 'But do it away from the door. We don't want blood everywhere.'

Sverr was still sitting beside his basket of haddocks. The fish slithered feebly one on another, and gaped, and choked slowly in the dry April air.

John set the bewildered piglet on its feet in the yard. He took a knife out of his belt and pushed the blade into the pink throat. The beast squealed. It ran and staggered, and the blood welled out of it. It stood still, then shook its head in a sad puzzled way. Blood spattered on the paving-stones. The boar's eye clouded, it keeled over, and it died in floods of gore.

'It will be a very tender pork pie,' said John the herdsman.

'What's happening out there at all?' said Ingerth from her loom.

Gudrun hung the fourth chicken from the rafters by its feet. She took a straw basket from the recess and went out into the yard. The two men, Sverr and John, were playing some kind of a game on the pavement, tossing flat stones into a circle scratched on the farthest flagstone. Gudrun crossed over the field to the mill. She had to bake a great quantity of bread and cakes for the feast that evening. The two greatest men in Orkney were to be the guests at the table: the Earl Magnus (Thora's son) and the Earl Hakon. She would have to excel herself. Thank goodness, some of the farm girls would be coming in in the afternoon to help in the kitchen. The ale, she thought; the ale at least will be very good. She had made it a month ago, in the cold hard air of March, always the best time for brewing. The ale had been seething gently for three weeks in barrels beside the kitchen fire. The earls would be glad of Gudrun's ale after their journey from the island, at sunset.

The little bell above the chapel at the end of the Hall began to nod and cry, and the bronze mouth brimmed with sound. *The Lord is risen! The Lord is risen! The Lord is risen!*

Ljot the stable-boy tugged at the bell-rope. The upsurge lifted him to his toes, again and again.

The Mass was over. A tall woman came out of the church, and after her a few farm women. She walked purposefully towards the door of the Hall. The priest told the stable-boy to stop ringing the bell so hard – he would have his arms out of their sockets, he would crack the bronze. The women from the farms smiled. Sverr the fisherman and John the herdsman threw their splintered stones into the grass and rose to their feet as the woman approached. 'The Lord is risen,' said the lady Thora, the widow of Erlend Earl of Orkney, to the two men. They mumbled the same greeting to her. Thora passed into the Hall. 'The Lord is risen,' she said in the interior gloom and coldness.

Ingerth, working at her loom, did not reply.

Gudrun crossed back over the field from the mill carrying a basket of new meal on her shoulder. 'The Lord is risen,' she greeted the women who were returning now from the Easter service to this croft and that fishing bothy. They raised their hands and answered, 'The Lord is risen, Gudrun.'

The lady Thora put a silver piece into the palm of Sverr's hand. 'Thank you, my lady,' said the fisherman, 'it is too much.' His tarry fist shook with greed and joy.

'No,' said Thora, 'but I have never seen such firm bright haddocks.'

Gudrun set down her oatmeal on the table. The kitchen was hot and full of the smells of blood and strangulation. The ale seethed gently in the barrels and gave out a sweet smell. Gudrun added some peats to the fire. 'The Lord is risen,' she said to the thin black cat that was stretching itself beside the new flames. Gudrun took a sharp knife and went out to the yard to gut the fish. The cat, smelling the dead salt creatures, ran after her, mewling faintly.

The Hall precincts were empty now, except for the boy Ljot who was sitting in the grass looking up at the shivering silent bell.

Gudrun listened at the door between kitchen and hall. Her mistress was saying to Ingerth, whose loom still clacked and birred inside, 'The Lord is risen.'

Ingerth, her daughter-in-law, wife of Magnus the earl, said nothing.

'The Lord is risen,' said Thora in a hurt voice. 'Does that mean nothing to you? Of course it means nothing, if one does not see all the actions of Christ's life in the events of every day. Today in the island of Egilsay your husband and his cousin – the two earls – who have been on bad terms for years, they are holding a meeting. They are making a treaty. Does that mean nothing to you? Orkney that has been bleeding to death for many winters, that is dead in fact and laid in a hollow rock, Orkney is to be resurrected again this very day. Does that mean nothing to you?'

'I am dead also,' said Ingerth. 'I am dead here in your house. I lie dead every night in your son's bed. I think I will never come to life again. All that talk means nothing to me.'

'The bread was broken in the church this morning,' said Thora. 'Here, tonight, in this very room, it will be broken again: the bread of peace. Does that not gladden your heart?'

'Nothing gladdens the heart of a married virgin who is growing old,' said Ingerth, and sent the shuttle flying again with fierce clackings.

Soon, from the kitchen fire, came the smell of baking bread.

Five farm girls came in the afternoon to help Gudrun in the kitchen and the house. One swept the floor of the main chamber; one scrubbed the great table; one ran and fetched for Gudrun, a little salt from the stone in the cupboard, a few dock-leaves from the ditch to keep the fish cool; one watched the fire anxiously, bringing in peats from time to time and stirring the flames; Solveig would have been better biding at home – she stood between the hearth and the kitchen bench gossiping like a bird all afternoon, yet Gudrun did not reprove her because it was such a special day, Easter Monday, and in the evening, here in Holm, the feast of the reconciled earls.

'The Lord is risen,' the girls murmured to each other from time to time, passing with broom or salt or flame or fish-oil. 'The Lord is risen.'

'. . . And so I just said to him,' said Solveig, '"Peter," I said, "you needn't bother coming back here, I don't want to see you again, what about the silver ring I gave you, what about my three pearls I found in the oysters, what have you done with them, drunk them most like, now I know it only too well, you've been coming here all winter to this house for only one thing, but now I've had enough, you can go some place else, what do you take me for, a simpleton," I said. And the last I saw of him he was going round the corner of the pigsty like a kicked dog, but the ale-house had the story the same night, and the brute was getting pots of beer for telling it over and over again . . .'

'The Lord is risen,' whispered little Una to the lady Thora as she passed her in the main doorway. Una was carrying in bits of greenery for the garnishing of the fish once they were baked.

'Indeed the Lord is risen,' said Thora to herself as she walked in her thick coat through the fields towards the shore. 'The whole world is alive and astir with resurrection. Look at the new grass in the ditch, how young it is and full of sap, and the wild flowers everywhere, and the birds dropping back among the islands from the fires of Africa.'

She passed some peat-cutters, a man and two women, on the hill. 'The Lord is risen,' said the women humbly as the lady of the Hall went past, but the man turned his back and sank his blade viciously into the soft spongy turf. 'Get on with your work,' he whispered to the women. 'Do you want to be warm next winter? It's all right for her – she gets her peats dug and dried for her, yes, and set on the fire, yes, and the ashes raked in the morning. She can walk about in the sun if she wants to. But the likes of us, we have to work our guts out for everything we have . . .' He spat on his hands. The two women clucked at him reprovingly.

'The very light is renewed at this time of year,' said Thora to herself as she walked on towards the shore. 'The air is no longer shroud-grey. There's a brightness in the wind. And the stars are not so fierce as in winter. There's a sweetness in that great wheel of a moon as it goes through the sky on an April night.'

A man ploughing behind an ox in the field below raised his hand and shouted, 'The Lord is risen, my lady.' Thora stopped and answered, 'The Lord is risen,' and passed on down to the beach where a few fishermen were sitting beside their sheds working with hooks and creels . . . Behind her, in a fold of the hills, Tolk the ploughman fell to cursing his ox; but even the cursings sounded new-minted, and they diminished at last to a few remote bright fragments.

Thora stood with her feet among the weeded washed rocks. At her approach the fishermen had turned their backs, not out of discourtesy but because they were shy in the presence of the great lady. They knitted their creels and baited their lines with great concentration. A lamb fluttered among the dunes; the ewe called to it from the edge of a low crag.

'At this time of year,' said Thora to herself, 'new life appears everywhere on the earth – lambs, calves, grice, nestlings. The new creatures come trooping through the door of spring. Heaven has ordained everything with great wisdom. Only man, the prodigal, is littered at all seasons of the year. How strange that is. Christ, as if to emphasize his manhood, chose to place his death at this time of birth and quickening; but at once, three days afterwards, he asserted his godhead by bringing out of death this thing that is so much more marvellous than birth even – resurrection. The whole earth and sea today is shaken with resurrection . . . Halcro,' she called to the oldest fisherman, 'thank you for the haddocks. Sverr brought them to the Hall. They are good fish. The Lord is risen. I am expecting Earl Magnus and Earl Hakon from Egilsay round about sunset.'

'They will come by road, my lady,' said Halcro. 'I hear there are horses waiting on the shore at Tingwall.'

That, thought Thora, was how they would come indeed. She was standing among her fishermen at one end of this large island that was called the Island of Horses – Hrossey. Earl Magnus and Earl Hakon would, after their kiss of peace on the island of Egilsay, cross over in a small boat to the shore of Tingwall. Their squires would have been waiting since morning with the horses. Tingwall and

Paplay were at opposite ends of the Island of Horses. The earls would have a long ride from Tingwall to the shore of Firth, then across the flank of Wideford Hill to the village of Kirkwall with its little church of St Olaf. They would stop there most likely for refreshment – a cup of wine and some honeyed bread – with the priests, then on again along the seabanks above Scapa Flow, until in the thickening light they saw below them the Hall of Paplay with its festive lights and flames.

'There will be happiness in Orkney after today,' said Thora to the old man.

Alternatively the two earls might sail from Egilsay, past the flat island of Wyre, then between Gairsay with its one hill and the long sprawl of Shapinsay, and avoiding Kirkwall and the priests sail through The String and drop anchor in the sheltered bay at Inganess. There they could get horses at a farm, and ride between the heather and the little bird-haunted hill lochs. In either case, the final stage of the journey would have to be by horse.

The lady Thora thought for a while, between the shining April sea and the ploughlands, of the skill and toughness and patience of the island generations. Hundreds of years ago men had come hungry to these islands, easterlings, and they had hauled up their longships here and at a score of other bays and inlets, and they had turned their salt sinewy hands to the earth. They had hewed cornerstones and set them here and there along the shore. They had dug little fields out of the heather. In summer they turned their axes against the dark aboriginal folk who lived among the hills. Harvests came, a good one this year, an indifferent one that year; and their beasts multiplied and their beasts dunged the earth and their beasts were struck down before winter. The families made alliances, quarrelled, schemed; and love blossomed here and there, erratic and marvellous. Somehow that Scandinavian tribe learned to live at reasonable peace, the farmer on the hill with the farmer at the lochside (though the women at the hearths were forever stirring up jealousies and ambitions and old angers). Or if a field here or there was desperately disputed, the litigants took it to the district assembly, and generally abode by the verdict of the men sitting solemnly on the side of the little hill. There were occasional spear-storms and corn-batterings; but in spite of that life had gone on, with new fields dug out of the hill year after year, and new poems sung to the harp, and new innocent eyes opening to the sun. There was a feeling of slow continuous ripening, generation by generation, as of corn waving sunwards through a long summer of history. The time of the great Earl Thorfinn – grandfather of Magnus and Hakon – seemed now, looking back, like a golden harvest, with all the sanctity and song and heroism that were in the islands at that time.

After the death of Earl Thorfinn it was as if a chill wind blew in from the sea, and the sun shrank. The horses reared their hooves at the grey sun beyond the equinox. Winter came early with its frosts and fires; that is to say, looking at these matters in the long perspective of history, for the past two generations life in the islands had not been so agreeable as it had been up to then. Spite, anger, upset in every island, in every district, in every household – a sense of stagnation and loss, of a honeycomb broken and the sweetness draining away.

What had happened? Some argued that it was simply a loss of independence and identity. The King of Norway had asserted all too successfully his overlordship of the islands (as he had not dared to do in Earl Thorfinn's time), and to emphasize it had set up two puppet earls to squeak and gesture at each other; for he knew that a single strong ruler in Orkney could, with a cynical half-nod eastwards, plough his own furrow and fill his own barns. So much was true: the lady Thora knew well enough how it had been with her own husband Erlend, yoked impotently in the earldom along with his brother Earl Paul. In those days the yawls had begun to rot along the shore. But matters had got much worse under the double rule of Magnus Erlendson and Hakon Paulson – war had broken out – all Orkney was sundered into two hostile camps, and foreign mercenaries rode through the cornfields all one summer – there was everywhere a sense of hopelessness and futility.

If misfortune goes on for too long – if stones drift over the mouth of springs and people no longer have the will to shift them – then one has a sense of other than purely political forces at work; a veiled mysterious cipher has entered the equation; Fate has taken a hand in the game.

As year on year of murder and bad faith and anarchy succeeded one another, it seemed that an evil winter indeed was deepening over everything. The islanders trembled at the approach of the black solstice. They knew well enough in theory how the disorder could be cured: if they had a single strong earl standing in the door of his palace up there in Birsay, guarding the heraldry and the music and the lawbook and the looms inside.

But now events had passed out of their control. They could do nothing about the evils around them. Fate was working out its own dark inscrutable design, which seemed to involve the death of Orkney. The mere mention of the word 'fate' increased the hopelessness and helplessness.

Indeed (thought Thora as she walked back home through the fields) the ancient faith continues to be strong here in the north. Men acquiesce too easily still in the orderings of Fate. They have had Christianity for more than a hundred years and they are not comfortable with the new religion. It has not entered into the bloodstream of the tribe at all. Well, today in Egilsay the new faith was being put to the test. The Orkneymen would see soon enough what a miraculous strength would flow from this meeting of enemies in Egilsay. It would be finally proven to them that it is Christ that rules the universe.

Even a pagan might feel on a day like this that the islands were astir with hope and expectation and promise. The Lord is risen. The dove is fallen and furled in Egilsay now, thought Thora. The meeting is over. The reconciled horsemen are on the road to Paplay.

As she drew near the Hall she saw two of the farm girls – Gudrun's helpers – bringing the slaughtered piglet from a hook on the courtyard wall to the fires inside. The beast had a dark gash at its throat . . .

At the shore, the crew of *Godspell* still sat among their creel-stones and twine. It was the first afternoon that year that they had been able to sit out of doors.

'She's a good kind lady,' said old Halcro reverently. 'God help her.'

'A fine sight it'll be,' said his son Harold, 'the two earls on the road, and all the gentry of Orkney riding behind them. From the ale-house door we might get a glimpse of them.'

'There'll be music and feasting till all hours,' said another fisherman.

'I'll tell you what the best sight of all would be,' said a young fisherman called Ward. (His father had lost all his fields and his steading in the troubles, and Ward had had to beg the fishermen for a place in their boat.) 'I'll tell you what the best sight of all would be – one horseman on the road tonight, a hard solitary silent man.'

The fishermen looked at Ward and shook their heads. They did not know what he was talking about.

In the Hall kitchen the preparations were almost over. There was a heap of baked haddocks on a platter at one side of the fire; on the other the huge pot of chicken broth steamed. One of the girls turned the young pig on the spit. The first of the ale had been poured into a silver jug and it had a tilted cap of froth. Gudrun's face was flushed. The lady Thora entered from the main chamber. Her hair hung loose. Some new idea must have occurred to her in the middle of her toilet.

The sun had been down over Hoy for ten minutes or more.

'Solveig,' said Thora, 'you've done little but chatter nonsense all day. Go out and listen for the sound of hooves. They'll be riding between Gaitnip and Deepdale. It's a calm evening. You'll be able to hear them miles off.'

Solveig put on her shawl and went outside.

The pig on the spit rained drops of its own burning fat into the fire.

'Una,' said Thora, 'have you set the ale-horns, a dozen of them, on the table?'

'Yes, I have,' said Una, 'and I polished the silver bits round the rims too.'

'Well, don't stand there gaping – carry the goblet through,' said Thora.

From the main chamber came the slow irregular clack of the shuttle. The lady Ingerth had been at her weaving all day, and still she sat at the loom in the fading light, plotting intricacies of form and colour. She mingled scarlet thread with black thread and grey thread. It was uncertain yet what the web was meant to represent.

'The priests in Kirkwall are keeping them,' said Thora.

'That's what it is. Meantime the fish is getting cold. Magnus said they would be here before sundown, for sure . . . Gerda.'

'Ma'am,' said Gerda.

'Go out and stand on the howe. You have good eyesight. See if you can see them.'

'It's getting dark, ma'am,' said Gerda.

'Just do what I say,' said Thora. 'Keep your eyes on the road. If you keep looking you'll see a thicker moving clot of shadows on the hillside. That will be them.'

Gerda took her flushed face into the darkening wind outside.

'There's two or three good ale-houses between Tingwall and here,' said Gudrun, between innocence and mockery.

'Earls are not blacksmiths and poachers,' said Thora. 'Earls don't go into ale-houses.'

Solveig Rattle came back out of the night, shivering. 'There's no sound of horses on the road at all,' she said. 'I crouched there five minutes with my ear to the ground.'

The loom fell silent next door.

'I've heard,' said little Una to Broda, breaking the new bread with her fingers and arranging the pieces on a platter, 'I've heard that that Earl Hakon is a terrible man. Of course I've never really set eyes on him. But they say he's fierce and black as a wolf.'

'That's nonsense, Una,' said Thora. 'Earl Hakon is a very gentle courteous person. You'll see that for yourself before the night's done. Broda, my hair.'

'Maybe, Una,' said Solveig, 'he'll take you on his knee.'

'O for the love of God,' shrieked Una. 'I would die!'

Gerda came back, cold and grey-faced. She squatted beside the fire and held her hands out to the blaze. 'The road's empty, ma'am,' she said. 'There's nothing moving in the darkness but a cow and a few fishermen going up from the beach to the ale-house.'

'It could be,' said Gudrun, 'that the meeting took longer than they thought. Maybe they didn't get away from Egilsay till late.'

Broda stood on tiptoe behind Thora. She pushed the comb into the burnished coils of hair and fastened it with a pin.

'That's possible,' said Thora. 'That's likely, in fact. They were hard and difficult, the things they had to discuss. If only Magnus and Hakon had been there themselves, just the two of them, it would all have been so much more simple. But there were men in Egilsay today – Sighvat Sokk for example, and Hold Ragnarson – awkward difficult creatures at any time – supposed to be councillors – they couldn't counsel a cock to crow . . .'

'There will be a wish-bone for everybody,' said Gudrun to Una and Broda. 'Don't quarrel about it.'

Through the open kitchen door the first star shone above the hill.

'Whatever delay there has been,' said Thora, 'Magnus and Hakon are coming to Holm. Nothing will stop them. It was a promise. They'll come, I know it. They'll come if it should be midnight.'

'This pig will be a cinder long before midnight,' said Gudrun. She took her forearm across her shining brow.

The dog set up a sudden fearful unending hullabaloo at the gate: until the stable-boy ran out and silenced him.

'Listen,' said Una.

The women stood about the open door. They tilted their heads. They touched their fingers to their ears. They heard breathings in the night, a distant whinny and snicker, thuds on the soft turf, the bright faint chime of harness. A troop of horsemen was abroad. A horn blew. As if the rising sea rolled stones upon rock there was a sudden outbreak of clops and splashes – the horsemen were crossing the burn half a mile away. The women heard Ljot calling, 'This way, this way – follow the lantern.' The night was one jangling snorting onset then, though the hooves fell muted again on the grass of the park: a tumult of thuds and breathings, coming closer. 'This way, my lord,' said Ljot. 'Take care of the duck-pond.' Iron on stone: the cobbled courtyard was loud with men and horses. 'The stable is over here,' cried Ljot. 'I'll hang the lantern in the rafters. There's plenty of hay. There's water in the trough over there.'

'It's them,' cried Solveig, clapping her hands. 'They've come!'

'Come back inside, all of you,' said Thora. 'Shut the door. Gudrun, see to the ladling of the soup. I don't want any carry-on tonight between women and horsemen. Remember what day it is. When I sound the bronze, that will be the time to put the fish on the plates. Una, come with me, please.'

Thora opened and closed the door between kitchen and dining chamber. Una followed her. Ingerth had left the loom and was pacing unquietly between the hearth and the table.

'Your husband is here,' Thora said. 'Get ready. I should put on something gay – that yellow gown for example . . .' She passed on, followed by Una, into her bed-chamber.

The clatter of hooves lessened in the courtyard as the horses were led one by one from the troughs to the flickering stable. To the girls watching from the kitchen the yard was a throng of noisy shadows. One tall shadow detached itself from the clamour. It moved, slow and hesitant, towards the stone heraldry of the main door. A fist rose and fell.

Ingerth in her sombre dress stood behind the loom and

did not stir in the direction of the vibrant oak.

Thora, fixing a silver brooch to the shoulder of the red magnificence swathing her, came breathless out of her room towards the summons, followed by Una.

'Welcome,' she said. And pulled the heavy door open.

A solitary figure reeled in, and stood there, rooted, shaking his head slowly in the light. Thora and Ingerth recognized, through the ale-stupor and the mask of fatigue, Hakon Paulson, the second of the two expected guests.

'I've come, Thora,' he said. 'I'm here.'

'You're welcome, Hakon,' said Thora. She moved towards him anxiously. He bent his barley-reeking head. Thora kissed him on the cheek. 'The Lord is risen,' she said.

'From Egilsay to here was a long hard journey,' said Hakon thickly. 'I've had one or two rough journeys in my time. This was the worst.'

'Sit down, Hakon,' said Thora. 'You're very tired.'

Hakon took his axe from his belt and laid it on the table. He sat down with tipsy suddenness in the high chair. His face was carnival red among the torches. 'Yes,' he said, 'I'm tired. There was a lot of business to do in Egilsay today.'

'So,' said Ingerth. The shifting fire-reflections went over her and filled with shadows her cheeks and temples and throat. Her face fluttered slowly in the fire-and-torch-light. Her black eyes never left Hakon's face.

'I came as quickly as I could,' said Hakon. 'We had trouble with the horses. One cast a shoe. They turned their heads away, anywhere but in this direction. The horses did not want to come to Holm. One broke his leg on Wideford. They had to finish him off.'

'Hakon,' said Thora, 'it looks to me that you've been celebrating early.'

'No,' said Hakon, 'but I do not like killing. The horse – it was Sigurd's gelding – he stumbled on a loose stone on the side of Wideford. We had to kill him. That kept us back.'

There was silence in the Hall. From the kitchen came the clatter of pots and the cold swift orders of Gudrun to the farm-girls. Little Una stood at the door between hall and kitchen, waiting for the word to bring in the soup.

'The dinner is almost ready,' said Thora. 'You must be hungry, Hakon.'

'No,' said Hakon. 'I want to drink.'

'Una,' said Thora, 'tell Gudrun that we do not want the soup or the fish just yet. Tell her to fill a jug with the oldest strongest ale – the stuff she brewed for Christmas.'

Una disappeared into the hot clattering kitchen.

'So, what is keeping Magnus so long out in the stable?' said Thora.

Una came from the kitchen carrying the silver goblet. She set it carefully on the table before Thora. Thora tilted the jar into a cup. The ale went over thick and frothy and dark. She handed the cup to Earl Hakon. 'Magnus is not in the stable,' said Earl Hakon. 'Magnus is in Egilsay.' He drank till the beard on his upper lip was dark and soaking. He noticed Ingerth standing between the loom and the hearth fire. 'Madam,' he said, 'your husband Earl Magnus is in Egilsay. Magnus couldn't come to Holm tonight.' He drank again. 'This is very good ale,' he said.

'It is all one to me,' said Ingerth, 'where he is.'

'Una,' said Thora, 'pour some more of the ale into the earl's cup.'

Una poured out of the jug. Her hands shook. The horn shook. Some ale fell on Hakon's fist.

'You stupid girl!' cried Thora. 'Have you never learned to pour straight out of a jug!'

Una's lower lip quivered and she set the empty jug on the table. 'I'm sorry,' she whispered to Earl Hakon.

'No,' said Hakon, 'but it was my arm that was shaking. What's your name, girl?'

'Una.'

'You are a very pretty girl, Una. I'm sure you're a great help to the lady Thora. It was my fist that was shaking.'

'Yes, lord,' said Una.

'Una,' said Thora, 'the jug is empty. Ask Gudrun to fill it up again from the same barrel.'

'Yes,' said Una, and lifted the empty jug from the table.

'Tell Gudrun,' said Thora, 'that we will not be needing food after all. Tell her the girls are to carry the food to the men in the stables.'

'Keep coming back with the ale jug,' said Hakon. 'You are a good girl.'

'So Magnus is staying tonight in Egilsay,' said Thora.

'That's right,' said Hakon. 'In Egilsay. Magnus is staying tonight in Egilsay.'

'What house, I wonder?' said Thora. 'Will he be sleeping in some farm, or at the priest's house?'

'No house,' said Hakon. 'I wish that girl would hurry with the ale. He is spending the night in the fields.'

Una came back with the goblet and set it on the table, and stood looking with wide eyes at Earl Hakon.

'Go back to the kitchen,' said Thora sharply to Una. 'The earl and I have important things to talk about.'

'You are a very sweet pretty girl,' said Hakon. Thora poured ale into Hakon's cup. Una went back into the kitchen. Ingerth twisted her ring, a glittering golden snake-writhe, on her finger: she looked at Hakon indifferently.

From the yard and the stable came sounds of laughter, a mingling of bright and dark cries. The women were offering fish and bread and cheese to the men who had ridden from Egilsay. A woman broke the chickens into hot pieces. A woman put a knife into the roast pig. There were cheers when a girl crossed the yard with her arms full of ale-horns. The horses nuzzled the hay. Solveig shrieked twice. There were volleys of dark and bright cries. The main barn was a house of laughter.

Earl Hakon put the ale cup to his mouth and emptied it with several strong workings of his throat. 'This is very good ale,' he said. 'I congratulate you. I'll tell you something. I am not a coward but I was terrified to come to this house tonight. What were we talking about?'

'Magnus in Egilsay,' said Thora.

'Magnus is not staying in any house,' said Hakon. 'Magnus is spending the night under the stars.'

'It will be cold for him,' said Thora. 'He did not take his thick coat with him.'

'No,' said Hakon, 'he is not needing any coat. Magnus will never need another coat. But I need more ale.'

'So,' whispered Ingerth. 'It is the dark bride.'

'Hakon,' said Thora, 'I think you've had plenty of that ale. You would be better of something to eat.'

'No meat,' said Hakon. 'I carved flesh in Egilsay today. I was hellishly sick after it.'

'Your axe is clean enough,' said Thora.

'It was Ofeig's axe,' said Hakon. 'I didn't do anything personally, if you understand. Lifolf the cook, he did it. You know Lifolf the cook? We put Ofeig's axe into his hands. Lifolf carved the meat.'

There was another long silence in the hall: the man building round his day's work a labyrinth of drunkenness – an old woman stumbling down dark hints and guesses to a simple central event (a fire on a stone, a lustration, a dove-fall). Ingerth looked at the web in the loom. It was grey lamb's wool, lightly woven, a half-finished summer coat: that would never now be worn.

Hakon poured a cup of ale for himself with a steady hand.

'Still you haven't told me what happened in Egilsay today,' said Thora.

Hakon drank deeply.

'A man died,' he said. 'That's what happened. A man died.'

'Well,' said Thora, 'that's always happening. Men die. Never a day but a man dies in this island or that. So long as this dead man in Egilsay was shriven and given heavenly bread for his journey, then he's happy enough, I'm sure. So long as he's lying in the church in Egilsay, between the font and the altar, all's well with him. The living weep – a mother, a widow, children weep – but there's worse things than a good death.'

'There were no children in this case,' said Ingerth.

'The dead man,' said Hakon, 'he is not in the church. He is in the fields. He is lying under the stars. I told you.'

'It is a work of mercy,' said Thora, 'to give the dead sanctuary and burial. What were you all thinking of in Egilsay today? There is more ale in the jug. Were you all so busy with peace-making that you had no time to carry this poor man who died into the kirk?'

Hakon kneaded his eyes with his fists. He bent his head on the table beside the ale jug. A convulsion, like a slow ponderous wave, passed through his body, from chest to knees. His face streamed. He opened his mouth. He yelled once, like a beast under a branding iron.

'Well wept, butcher,' said Ingerth.

Thora lifted one huge trembling fist from the table and stroked it. 'Well now,' she said, 'when you think of it there's worse places for a dead man to lie than the fields. But still I would be better pleased if the wounds and the silence were laid before the altar in the kirk of Egilsay. It isn't much for an old woman to ask.'

Hakon whimpered that he would send word to the priest and people of Egilsay in the morning. He sat up. He said in a firm voice that he was very tired. He said he must be on his way now. He thanked them for the fire and the ale. But still he sat where he was.

Thora touched him on the shoulder. He rose blindly to his feet. She kissed him again on his shivering mouth. She lit a candle from one of the wall torches. She called him 'son'. She led him through the far door to the bed-chamber beyond.

In the byres and the barn and the stables round the courtyard straw creaked and sang.

'The filth,' said Ingerth. 'The scum. The beast.'

On the half-finished cloth in the loom could be seen now, in the torchlight, a sun, a cornstalk, a cup.

BISHOP'S MOVE

ROBERT CRAMPSEY

THE BISHOP pressed his desk buzzer, and Mlle Hortense Pelissot came into his office from the cloistral reception area outside. Mlle Hortense had two qualities which made her an admirable appointments secretary for a bishop. She was meticulous in her work, and very few people survived the screening which decided whether they merited a personal interview with His Grace. The ungallant might have added a third quality for, with her sallow complexion, heavily bespectacled face and sagging, though corseted, figure, she was beyond the breath of scandal. Now, she stood primly in front of the large desk.

'Good morning, Monseigneur.'

'Good morning, Mlle Pelissot. I noticed you at Mass earlier, as ever.'

There had been perhaps fifty people at the seven o'clock Mass, and it was highly unlikely that the Bishop would not have noticed her as he distributed the Host, but it always pleased Hortense when he commented upon her presence.

'It makes a good start to the day, Monseigneur.'

'What better? Now, Mademoiselle, what have we today?'

'This morning, a visit from the Scout leader here in Basse-Terre, then a meeting with the treasurer and secretary of the St Vincent de Paul Society. Oh, and Soeur Marie Angélique requests a brief interview at about eleven.'

The Bishop groaned inwardly. It was scarcely for this that he had left his home in Limoges and proceeded to ordination via the Séminaire St Sulpice and the University of Louvain. Volunteering for service abroad, he had arrived in Guadeloupe to become the prop of a lingeringly-ill bishop. For four years he had virtually run the diocese, and had then been consecrated by the venerable Bishop of Guyane. His elevation to the bishopric had caused certain murmurings. He was a European in his mid-forties and a growing sector of opinion felt that a black bishop was overdue.

He was white – not only in skin but in dress, for he wore a snowy, full-length soutane, caped at the shoulders, with no personal adornments save a large, black pectoral cross and an inconspicuous agate ring. The only touch of colour was supplied by the merest glimpse of purple episcopal sock, connecting the white hem of the soutane to the sturdy black shoes.

'And this afternoon, Mademoiselle?'

'Blank, Monseigneur. There was a certain matter up near Deshaies . . .'

The Bishop grunted irritably. He regarded himself as liberal, but to discuss, even obliquely, the shortcomings of a fellow-priest with a layman, still more a laywoman, annoyed him more than he felt it reasonably should.

'The matter of Father Eugène Drollée,' went on Hortense with unwitting temerity.

'I remember, Mademoiselle,' said the Bishop heavily. 'Tell Father Paul I'll need him to drive me this afternoon. Don't tell him where he's going. I'll inform him myself. Only you and I know it's not Deshaies, and, as *I* won't tell anyone, Mademoiselle . . .' He left the last few words unspoken.

'I understand, Monseigneur.'

'When does our friend from Le Scoutisme appear?'

'He's here now, with two young Scouts. They have a new song they want to sing to you.'

'Charming. Give me two minutes and send them in.'

The Bishop leant back in his chair and surveyed the huge map of the island and its dependencies which covered an entire wall. The spiritual welfare of nearly 400,000 people lay in his hands. For 2000 of that number, he had taken a decision which would personally affect that spiritual welfare. He hoped he was right, but having taken counsel on earth and from heaven, he had made up his mind. St Augustine tells us that this is a good characteristic in a bishop.

The heavy, brass-studded door swung open and the three Scouts appeared escorted by Hortense, who then withdrew, but with protective, backward glances. Monseigneur exchanged greetings with the Scout leader, an earnest, brown-skinned young man of medium height, and evaded an over-pietistic attempt to kiss the episcopal ring.

'You have a song for me, boys?'

'Yes, Monseigneur.' It was the older and curlier of the two little black heads.

'What is it called, this song?'

'"May We Meet Again Together Round the Great Eternal Camp-fire", Your Grace.'

'A happy thought,' murmured the Bishop.

The young man raised his arm, pocked with badges of different colour and shape, and the two little boys sang in thin, tuneful voices. The Bishop allowed his eyebrows to quirk slightly when the youngsters carolled of an *indaba* with the Celestial Chief Scout, but he thanked the boys kindly. He asked one or two sensible questions about Scouting, such as, had the new uniform attracted more recruits, and at what age did young fellows feel the pull of the Scout Movement weaken. He resisted courteously, but very definitely, the Scout Leader's suggestion that Monseigneur should look in often on Tuesday nights to see for himself. He gave the boys fruit juice – and the Scout Leader, who spurned a proffered whisky with the conscious virtue of St Anthony rejecting a virgin in the desert. Monseigneur rang for Hortense, who removed the trio.

Left to himself, the Bishop smiled ruefully. Only a nation as determinedly anti-intellectual as the British could have produced such a movement. He implored forgiveness for his passing thought that more accurate Boer shooting at Mafeking might have saved the world a deal of tedium.

His talk with the officials of the St Vincent de Paul Society was more agreeable to him. True, the Society tended to attract the patronizing lawyer and schoolmaster, but it did relieve some genuine cases of poverty. The Bishop was not over-impressed by the argument that, increasingly, government social services were doing this job better. He saw the work of St Vincent's gentlemen as a practical application of 'Love thy neighbour'. They left, happy with an episcopal donation of 500 francs and permission to hold a collection in all the churches of the diocese on the second Sunday in April.

The Bishop took advantage of the lull before the Sister Marie Angélique storm to read his Office and then sip a fruit juice. Sister Marie Angélique was Mother Superior of the Pauline Congregation, and not the least of the Bishop's trials. A pretty woman, who wore the white habit of her Order with elegance, she had a most emphatic cast of mind and a taste for independence which she cloaked, half-humorously, under a guise of deep deference. The Bishop often reflected that the newspaper reports of women's liberation movements were nothing very novel. According to his predecessor, and in his own experience, Sister Marie Angélique had been liberated for years. She came in and, in response to his hand signal, sat down demurely.

'You are welcome to this house, Sister.'

'My lord Bishop, I am ashamed to add even a fractional weight to your heavy load. But it is my duty, or so I hold it, to seek your advice for our community. After all, you are our father in God.'

This was the Bishop's belief too, though there had been times when Sister Marie Angélique had given him cause to doubt it. He contented himself with saying, 'Bear ye one another's burdens, Sister. Did not the Good Shepherd carry the sheep on His Own shoulders? Our attention and advice are fully at your disposal.'

Sister Marie Angélique explained the reason for her visit very cogently and concisely. There had been discussions amongst the community, which had noticed from newspapers that sister houses in the USA had forsaken the long habits and for everyday wear the nuns there now dressed in white blouses, navy skirts and nylon stockings. They continued, of course, to wear the cross.

'If I understand you, Sister, you would like to follow the example of the good American sisters?'

'You do not approve, Monseigneur?'

'I am not sure, as yet. I have a certain fear that nuns who dress as you suggest will not remain in the religious life long. This was, I know, the thinking of His Grace the Archbishop of Los Angeles, when I spoke to him in Rome last year.'

'His Grace is known as a . . .'

'As a diehard, Sister? Perhaps. But he has some reason

in his wish that nuns should dress as nuns have dressed. The habit is largely for protection, and men are entitled to know – clearly, and at once – when a woman is a Bride of Christ.'

Sister Marie Angélique stirred slightly. 'Do you refuse your permission then, Monseigneur?'

'Let me think on it. I shall give you my answer when next I see you at the convent.'

'You will be coming up to hear our confessions next week, My Lord.'

'Of course, of course. I had forgotten Father Damian is on retreat, and that I must stand in for him.'

Hearing confessions at the convent was a difficult task for the Bishop. There was no anonymity, in that he always knew when Sister Marie Angélique was in the confessional. That he did was nobody's fault: it was merely that she was the only penitent who did not confess to sins of uncharitable thoughts against Sister Marie Angélique. He stood up, and accompanied the nun to the door, remembering to enquire after the health of Sister Jeanne d'Arc, who had been in a local sanatorium for the last few months with suspected pulmonary tuberculosis.

'We shall see you next week then, Monseigneur.'

'Surely. When you pray for Sister Jeanne, remember me also.' He went back into the office.

Two hours later, after a lunch for which he had no stomach, the Bishop sat beside Father Paul as the modest diocesan Citroën crept through the narrow streets of the island capital. The glare of the afternoon sun dazzled his eyes, the Coca-Cola and Pepsi signs, tacked to the low-fronted nineteenth-century houses, seemed more than usually tawdry. Father Paul, his timid attempts at chatter rejected, turned left down the rue Maurice Marie Caire towards the seafront. Almost opposite the great banana-wharf he swung right, on to the Boulevard du Général Charles de Gaulle and took the Baillif–Rocroy road. This was in response to a curt motion of the hand by the Bishop.

There was silence during the drive out past the tiny Baillif airstrip and on the road which wound round the west of Basse-Terre island. The car raised the slumbrous dust of Vieux-Habitants, and called forth feats of agility from the dogs and pigs of Bouillante. Where the road rose at the far end of the latter village, the Bishop quietly asked Father Paul to draw in to the side. He sat staring out to sea, but he was not looking at the Ilets à Goyaves or the two-toned ocean, aquamarine near the shore, cobalt stretched beyond. He was seeing the face of Father Eugène Drollée.

Few things are more distressing to a bishop than a priest whose conduct gives scandal. Father Drollée had been warned before that his liking for wine had moved from a convivial habit to a vice. He had started by drinking quietly on those evenings when the doctor was away from his village and down in Basse-Terre. He had, for a while, had a radio transmitter with which he raised radio hams all over the world, and the arrival of their call-sign cards was the high point of his week. Then his housekeeper had carelessly caused an electrical fire which had badly damaged the R/T, and he lacked the money or heart to replace it.

So, he began to drink a bottle of an evening, and occasional custom turned to iron ritual. He began to have difficulty in turning out for sick calls. A frightened child from one of the hamlets on the Little Plain or Big Plain rivers would pour out an entreaty for the priest to come. He, tall, thin, stooping, would brush a sparse lock of his greying hair from over his eye and stand, his smile half-kind, half-foolish.

For a time he made the calls, though with difficulty. Then he missed one, fatally, soon another. The Bishop first spoke lovingly to him, later rebuked him in charity, and finally sent him on retreat to the Benedictine monastery in Martinique.

Father Drollée returned and was welcomed. This, too, disturbed the Bishop; the parishioners had never ceased to love this frail, flawed priest. All seemed well. And then – morning Mass grew later, although always said with great decorum, and if a parishioner took sick after sunset, the zeal of the neighbouring curé of Pointe-Noire might alone stand between him and an unprovided death.

The Bishop stirred. A bad priest must be cast out lest, in giving scandal, he drive others from the Church. But was Father Eugène Drollée a bad priest? He drank, his house-keeper was young and unnecessarily pretty, but she lived at the other end of the village and had never been known to remain after dark. There was no taint of immorality, for had there been, the Bishop well knew that he would have heard of it long before now.

'Come on then, Father,' he said grimly to Father Paul, and the young priest obediently put the car in gear. Ten minutes later they stopped in the village where this worrying priest had the care of souls.

The church was stone-faced, low, without a steeple, the windows and door in the Roman style. It stood on a raised ledge of rock facing across the road to the sea. The faithful, emerging from the front door, were greeted by the sight of the war memorial, rather unusual in that the obligatory angel was replaced by the wooden effigy of a French soldier of revolutionary times. The style of the image was that of a ship's figurehead.

The nautical décor was carried on inside and outside the church. The two lamps which lit the dusty path that bisected the dispirited grass were port and starboard lights, coloured as such. Inside, the wooden benches were arranged in an arrow formation, rather than one behind the other. The altar table was a slab of marble placed on a tree trunk. The burnished sanctuary lamp flickered perpetually, suspended from an ox-yoke which spanned the altar. Next to the baptimsal font stood a breath-taking model of a fully-rigged brigantine. It would have been hard to find a church which more perfectly breathed the essence of the community which it served.

The Bishop and Father Paul genuflected, knelt, said a brief prayer and left by a side door which took them across a red-earth courtyard to the parish-house. It was only slightly better than the neighbouring *cases* and the episcopal eye took in the square of plywood which plugged a hole in the corrugated iron roof and the sack containing a large number of wine bottles which stood near the church wall on a bare patch of earth.

Father Drollée himself answered the door. If he were surprised, he gave no sign of it and eagerly welcomed his unbidden guests. He offered goat's cheese and bananas, apologizing for the poverty of his table. The Bishop, who had seldom been less hungry, accepted a banana to avoid an unpardonable breach of manners, remarking that His Master had often fared less well. It was a tribute to the man that, on his lips, there was nothing sententious about the remark.

The three clerics talked generally for ten minutes or so, while they drank the coffee the housekeeper prepared for them. Ladylike, the Bishop thought, distinctly ladylike. Then he dispatched Father Paul on an errand to the priest of Pointe-Noire, much to the young curate's chagrin, for he suspected the purpose of the visitation and was not exempt from normal human curiosity. He knew better, though, than to demur.

The Bishop came immediately to the task which his duty laid upon him.

'I have to tell you, Father, that I must ask you to leave the diocese and return to France.'

The priest's mouth tightened fractionally but his face was composed as he asked, 'May I know why, Monseigneur?'

'I think we both know why, Father. Late Masses, sick calls unanswered, indecorous behaviour in public and private.'

'With all submission, Monseigneur, I have to tell you that I have never failed to say my daily Mass yet.'

'I am sure you have not. I am equally sure that your time of starting Mass varies from day to day as the date of Easter does from year to year.'

'Does it matter, if Mass be said?'

'You should not have to ask that. A cane-cutter going to the fields, a woman on her way to market or with meals to make, cannot wait until a priest is sufficiently sober to stand before the altar of God without disgracing himself and shaming his congregation.'

'Monseigneur, no one here could say that I ever offered the Holy Sacrifice while in a drunken state, or that I ever said Mass with anything but the greatest reverence for the rubrics.'

'I know this too, Father Eugène. Had it been otherwise, you would not be sitting here at this moment.' The Bishop leaned forward. 'However – the inescapable fact, Father, is that you drink, and will continue to drink. There is a sack of bottles out there which is a reproach to your priesthood.'

The priest offered a timid sally, 'Just dead men, my lord, just dead men.'

'Then it's a comfort to know that at least *they* didn't die without the aid of the priest.'

A red patch appeared on Father Drollée's cheeks, for all the world as if his face had been slapped hard. The Bishop, sensing his advantage, pressed the stricken priest hardly.

'You think that is a terrible thing to say, Father, that I sin against charity? Maybe I do. If so, it is to draw to your attention the awesome responsibility you carry as a priest. To miss a sick call is to send a man out of the world to the possibility of eternal damnation. It is the dereliction of duty which I pray most fervently to be spared.'

'But, Monseigneur,' humbly, 'are we not told that man may attain Heaven by instant personal repentance?'

The Bishop looked thoughtful, and quoted:

'Betwixt the stirrup and the ground,
Mercy I asked, mercy I found.

Your English poet may be right, although I have never found that race to be of an especially theological turn of mind.' Then, more briskly, 'But as a priest, and indeed as a bishop, I would want to know that I had done my utmost to ease and solace a man's dying hours. There is nothing a priest does which compares in importance with that. As a bishop, I am bound to regard with abhorrence any failure to administer the last sacraments.'

There was an intense silence in the shabby room. The Bishop noted the scuffed and worn easy-chair, the wooden chair which lacked a spar. On the wall hung a garish calendar, conveying the compliments of the local garage. The only object of distinction was a neatly carved statue of St Yves, patron saint of lawyers. Breton loyalty extended even to their saints, the Bishop thought ruefully.

Father Drollée spoke suddenly:

'My lord, how would this removal be done?'

'I will contact the head of your Order in France. You will find a home at the mother house there; in time you might even return to parish work. Where there are more men of your intellect and interest, Father, you will be less likely to drink.'

'I should be a stranger in my own land, Monseigneur. Do you know how long I have been in Guadeloupe? Do you know that I regard it as my home?'

The Bishop steeled his voice slightly. 'I know that a priest has no home on earth. You and I have been homeless from the moment the Bishop laid his hands upon us. Do you imagine that I came to this decision lightly, that I indulge a whim?'

'No, Monseigneur.'

'I reviewed your whole career, Father. Eugène Drollée, born Rennes 1913, ordained priest 1937, came to Guadeloupe 1939. You have given thirty years of devoted service to this island, to these people.'

'Is not that worth something, Monseigneur?'

The Bishop checked his reply as the housekeeper appeared, to ask Father Drollée what she should leave for his supper. He waited until her lemon dress disappeared into the kitchen and he heard the door slam.

'It is worth a great deal, Father. That is why I am sending you away from here, before the love these villagers have for you turns to tolerance, and certainly before that tolerance turns to contempt.'

The kind, tired face of Father Drollée crumpled as he realized the fixity of the Bishop's mind. His fingers fumbled blindly with the oilcloth which covered the table. He threw in his last forces.

'If I were to be disciplined again, Your Grace, and

swear a firm purpose of amendment?'

The housekeeper looked in to say she was leaving, her work done for the day. The two men watched her cross the earth yard, then they listened to the diminishing click of her heels on the road.

The Bishop smiled an odd smile. It managed to convey genuine compassion and, at the same time, very finally to close the door.

'This would be your fourth firm purpose, Father. You deserve better of me.'

Father Drollée hunched his shoulders in misery. 'I am a failed priest. It is right that my disgrace should be public.'

'You do God an injustice, Father, if you think He will forget almost thirty years of loyal and loving service. He will remember that you spoke up for the small *colons* of this district when the big banana companies wanted their land. He will remember, too, that when the teacher in school took ill, you yourself taught the young children for almost a year.'

'They are men and women now, Monseigneur. I am sorry they are grown up to see that their priest is inadequate. Yet, it is just.'

There was the faintest suggestion of unease – never heartiness in a Bishop? – as his superior said, 'No question of disgrace, I assure you, Father.' Conscious of the difference in age, the Bishop could not bring himself to use the hierarchical 'My son'. 'It will be notified in the diocesan bulletin that reasons of health compel you to return to Europe. You may announce the same from your pulpit. On the Sunday before you go, I shall preach to your parishioners, to let them see how much your labours here have served the Church. I shall preach well, Father, for I shall believe what I say.'

There was the slide of tyres on the road outside. Father Paul was back. The Bishop opened the half-shuttered window, leaned out, and told him to wait in the car.

'Monseigneur, may I ask one thing?'

'You may ask, Father. I may answer.'

'I have heard in the village, I have read in the newspapers, that the government here wants to return all white priests to Europe and replace them with native curates. Is this perhaps why I am being asked to go?'

The Bishop fought against the tremendous temptation to tell the charitable lie. He conquered.

'No, Father, it has nothing to do with that. The government might like to do this – and I am certainly the last white Bishop – but the Church does not follow the dictates of any government in these matters. How many students are in the seminary here? I'll tell you, eleven. Of those, five may last the course. I have a constant fight with Rome to keep the seminary open.'

He saw the last shred of illusion fall from Father Drollée's face, and remembered that even a bishop must be a comforter, if he can.

'There will be a place for you in your Order still. Perhaps in the mother house in Paris, perhaps nearer your own Brittany. Have you any relations still there, Father?'

'A sister, widowed. I have not seen her since I was last in Rennes in 1947. To her, I am an abstraction to pray for, a cause to send money to occasionally, a source of quiet boasting to her friends. As a returned priest I should be in her way, I should make her feel uncomfortable.'

'It is difficult to talk naturally to a priest,' the Bishop mused aloud. 'Still more so to converse with a bishop, if my own experience is any guide.'

He leaned across the table earnestly. 'I am bound in duty, Father, to advise you of your rights in the matter.

You may write to your Superior-General, to the Apostolic Delegate, direct to Rome even. If you do, I shall be pleased rather than offended. I do not wish to incur the rightful anger of God for unjust procedure against a brother priest.' He paused. 'I ask you to let me know your decision within the week. I want the matter resolved within two or three months at most.'

'So soon! To decide, I mean. Monseigneur, I love these people, this village, this house, wretched as it must appear.'

'I know that. That is why I ask you to do the greatest service you will ever do for them.' He made preparatory movements for departure.

'We have evening Mass on Thursdays, Monseigneur,' Father Drollée said shyly. 'Not too many come, but dare we hope that you would assist?'

The Bishop smiled warmly. 'Thank you, Father, but I have a diocesan education council meeting this evening at eight. If there are to be any bishops in heaven, God will have to let them in for their stewardship, I fear, rather than their piety.'

He signalled to the patient curate in the car that he was coming.

'Father Paul will not speak to me for a week now,' he murmured. 'Still, that may not be all loss.'

He moved to the door, and made no attempt to withdraw his hand as Father Drollée kissed the ring.

'Goodbye, Father. Think of what I've said, and remember the courses open to you. Ask the parishioners to remember me at Mass, and my intentions.' He grinned, and, fleetingly, looked boyish. 'You'll tell me I say that to all the parish priests. Well – I do!'

He was gone, with the long-suffering Father Paul. The stooped priest stood on the church steps, watching the faint white dust cloud as the car receded. It turned a corner, for a few moments was heard and not seen, then it was not heard either. Father Eugène looked at his watch, then shuffled back to the house. An hour and a bit till evening Mass.

In a self-punitive mood he sat on the hard wooden seat, although the lumpy, greasy armchair was only fractionally more comfortable. His eye was drawn to the photograph on the cupboard, a curiously brown-tinted one. His group at the seminary, managing to suggest the 1930s even on the eve of ordination, and despite wearing their clerical blacks. His eyes lack-lustrely scanned the once-familiar faces. Then his head jolted back.

One of his classmates, Felix Nouillet, was Procurator of the Order and powerful in its counsels. Léon Matignon was known to stand high in the esteem of the Superior General. For the first time he was flicked by a spark of anger against the Bishop. He had nine times the service of the Bishop on the island, twenty times Monseigneur's knowledge of the people. Who had warned the Bishop against the mad scheme of preaching sermons in Creole to the people? Who had warned that the people would be insulted that the Word of God should be preached in *patois*, rather than the dignified French which they knew to be the proper medium? He had, and the outcome had thoroughly justified him. He began to think of making a fight of it, of summoning these powerful allies from the dulled photograph. Why should he not fight the Bishop? Make a case of it, he thought. Rome was not renowned for speed in these matters and a couple of years might well elapse before any decision was taken. And then, it might be in his favour. He remained stiffly seated on the chair until the tinny church bell warned him of the imminence of Mass and the need for vesting.

Father Drollée had been right when he told the Bishop that not too many people would be at the Mass. Through the half-open vestry door he counted perhaps a dozen and a half people scattered thinly over the church. There was Mam' Yvette who would say the rosary noisily and upset the congregation. Madame Pertilaine was there, as she had been every day since her husband's body was spewed up by the boiling surf a year ago. Old Louis from the marsh was there and Pierre-Aimé, the only man of full vigour. Pierre-Aimé was a cane-cutter, and an instance of the strange outcroppings of genuine piety that occur in the most unlooked-for places and people.

He nodded to his clerk, the tiny, waif-like Gilot, thirteen years old, of the grubby surplice and frayed red collar. Even at that, he had taken the cleaner of the two which hung from the old hatstand.

Gilot rang the handbell, the tiny congregation rose, as priest and server walked out. Father Eugène placed the chalice on the altar, opened the Missal at the prayers for the day, and began the Mass.

'My brothers and sisters, to prepare ourselves for the sacred mysteries . . .' As he said the words, he knew he would go. Few as they were, his brothers and sisters had stayed with him to the end of the road. He had an unusual sense of empathy with this poor, scattered handful, a strange feeling of joy that their spiritual battles would soon be fought by a stronger, worthier priest.

The young schoolteacher, Marie-Adèle, was a faithful attender at the evening Mass. She played the harmonium during the distribution of Communion and the meditation which followed. When the Mass had started, the fast-dropping sun had left patches of crimson on the wooden floor as it streamed through the plain glass. Now, although little more than half an hour had elapsed, the church was in semi-darkness. The two great bunches of red hibiscus on the altar were drained of colour, and the candles on the tall holders flamed cruel and bright against the glass plates which protected them from the ferreting little eddies of wind blowing off the sea through the front door.

Mademoiselle Marie-Adèle, who chose the hymns, switched on her desk-lamp to light the harmonium keys. She sat down, smoothed her frock, flexed her fingers and moistened her lips. Her nerves were as taut as if she were playing for one of the great organists of St Sulpice or St Severin.

Father Drollée took the eleven Hosts in the *ciborium*. Those wishing to take communion had each put a Host there. It was a practice which saved waste. The priest said the words of consecration which had never ceased to move him, took the Host himself, then went forward to the altar rails to meet the communicants.

High and clear rose the pure voice of Mademoiselle Marie-Adèle, soaring skywards as the wheezing harmonium remained resolutely earth-rooted. She was joined by the gruff quavering of old Louis, then, in instalments, by the others.

'Tu es bon berger,
O Seigneur
Rien ne me va manquer
O Seigneur.'

The thin sound floated over the roadway and died at the water's edge. The priest read the post-communion prayers, gave the blessing and informed them of the death of M. Lamentard, late of the parish, at Rouen. The green and red lights lit the skeleton congregation as it dispersed.

In the vestry, Gilot hung his surplice on the hatstand.

He shoved his old gym shoes into a chaotic cupboard from which spilled torn hymn-books, religious magazines, table tennis bats and assorted sashes. Father Drollée watched him with affection.

'Thank you, Gilot. Remember, seven o'clock tomorrow morning, sharp.'

'Yes, Father, I'll be there. Oh, Gautier says he can serve Sunday, eleven. Do you want to play chess tonight, Father?'

'No, Gilot, I can't let you beat me this evening. I have a letter to write.'

' 'Night then, Father.'

' 'Night, Gilot.'

The boy bounded off barefoot down the path.

Left to himself the priest locked away the sacred vessels, finished disrobing, then re-entered the house.

He sat down at the table to begin his act of spiritual submission. Almost without looking, he reached behind him for a bottle and a glass. He took a sharp draught, then began to write fluently, while the frozen high hopes of his seminarian classmates regarded him from across the room.

THE BLIND READING

CARL MACDOUGALL

MY FATHER, two uncles and an aunt in Canada, all in three years. Two had died within four days of each other. My grandmother said we never were a lucky family; someone had put a curse on us.

Everywhere life is full of heroism. I learned when someone went into a room alone, it was best to leave them. Our busy times lapsed into a silent semi-circle, staring at the fire. Sobbing. Strangers sat in their heavy coats, swallowing a stream of tea. Some old buddy would sigh, sigh and stare at me, shake her head, bite her lower lip, then mutter into her cup, 'Aye, he's like his father.' I knew what it caused.

'Go out and play, son.' But I wasn't to play with Toe Blair or the foul-mouthed Jackie Carson. Anyway, they wanted to be soldiers or cowboys. I didn't like pretending to be dead and was too soft for football. You'll get kicked, my grannie had told me, and I knew she was right. Books helped me escape, but there was a hard reality. Everyone looked wild, red-eyed and miserable. I believed the dead would never be left in peace.

Every Sunday, after lunch, we took the tram to Lambhill Cemetery. The afternoons were warm and clammy in uncomfortable clothes. Black was the colour. We walked from the terminus and there were always crowds of people.

Up the hill and round the bend an old lady read aloud from a Braille Bible. She sat on a wooden kitchen chair and whispered parables into her grey clothes. Her pepper-and-salt hair was tied in a bun at the back of her neck; stubby fingers read the pages, horizontally translating to lips that hardly moved. She was undisturbed by the chink of money in a shoe box at her feet. I was fascinated and could have watched for hours. It's rude to stare, I was told. But I thought she didn't know I was staring.

There was talk. Some said she lived in a mansion and a car collected her at night. Others maintained she wasn't blind at all, or had memorized one passage and repeated it over and over again.

I was an impatient gravetender, anxious to be back at the Bible. One time she wasn't there on our way home. After that I made sure we left early. When I saw a car I looked to see if she was in it, even if there was only the driver. She burgled my dreams. A blind voice read from the Bible and the darkness was no longer my friend.

On a summer Sunday, Toe, Carsie and I were bored. We kicked cans and lay up the park pretending to be explorers.

'If you want to be real explorers, I know where we can go,' I said.

We got money from bottles hidden for such an emergency and sang, laughing, on the tram. At the terminus we were quiet and alone.

'Where'll we go now?' said Carsie.

'C'mon back,' said Toe.

'I know where to go,' I said.

They trailed up the hill after me, kicking stones.

Round the corner I saw her and smiled at the discovery.

'It's just a woman,' someone said.

'She's blind and reads the Bible.'

'So what?'

I stood snared.

'He's daft,' said Toe. 'C'mon back.'

'. . . and taught them, saying, Blessed are the poor in spirit: for theirs is the kingdom of heaven. Blessed are they that mourn: for they shall be comforted. Blessed . . .'

Time was words and fingers and money. When the people were gone she closed the book, picked up the shoe box and turned her yellow and white eyes to the day. I wanted to talk, but there was a racing pulse and a heavy throat.

'What are you doing here, son?'

I turned, and saw the voice in a police car.

'Nothing.'

'Where do you stay?'

'Keppochhill Road.'

'Are you lost?'

Lost.

'You're a bit of a way away for a wee boy. We'll give you a lift. Get in the back.'

From the car I saw sightless eyes, staring, alone, a Bible and a shoe box full of money on her lap.

The policeman dropped me off at the foot of the road.

'You can make your own way home. We don't want to give your mother a fright, do we?'

Archie Wallace saw me first.

'Here he is. The daft explorer. Imagine going to see a daft old woman reading the Bible.'

The laughter was forced, loud and followed me, landing at the pit of my stomach.

That was the end. I did not know it, but time healed and memories darkened. A grey salve stopped us going to the cemetery. I never saw her again.

SPUD: SUFFERING THROUGH SUNDAY

WILLIAM GRANT

ON THE top landing of a grey, Glasgow tenement – constructed for the exclusive purpose of being a slum seventy years past, it had in no way relinquished its position – Beenie moved around the small kitchen in the constrained bursts of laboured activity she had grown accustomed to since passing her sixth month of pregnancy. The least movement seemed to require an effort of will equal to that she had always thought would be necessary for climbing Ben Nevis, which, although she had never personally seen it, filled her imagination whenever anything larger than the hills surrounding the city was mentioned.

What little furniture there was reflected the fashion of the previous decade. Two large armchairs, well worn; a table in the centre of the floor with four matching chairs; a wardrobe, a tallboy, a welsh-dresser and, looking strangely alien, her one concession to contemporary times – a large, expensive, colour television. At this moment, at thirty-four years of age, she felt as old as the building itself. And, to add to her troubles, she could hear him stirring behind the heavy curtains that served to screen-off the recessed-bed.

Further effort was now demanded. She waddled clumsily towards the stove. Lit the gas rings. Put on frying-pan and kettle. The bed creaked again; she endeavoured to hurry but could gain no more speed. Mushrooms, tomatoes, eggs, ham, she managed all of them into the pan, nauseated by their stench. Wanting to vomit but strongly repressing the urge in the firm knowledge that, since she had eaten nothing, she would spend an interminable period stooped over the sink retching.

Spud pushed aside the curtains and peered through into the daylight. 'How's the time?' he croaked.

'Your breakfast is on,' she replied. It having been some years since they had actually listened to each other with anything resembling intent interest.

'How's the time, I said?' He glanced about, his heavy-eyes and tousle-haired head disembodied by the curtains. 'Is there any beer left, what's goin' on inside my skull you wouldnae believe?'

'Hell mend you,' Beenie muttered indifferently. 'Get out of there till I get that bed spread, suppose somebody was to come in, you layin' there at this time of day!'

Since no one would have considered coming in this early on a Sunday morning the question was given the lack of response it seemed to deserve. Pouring out a pint mug of tea she handed it to him. An arm extended cautiously to join the head. He swallowed a mouthful, delighting in his agony as the scalding liquid seared the roof of his mouth.

'Where are the weans?' he questioned.

'Up and oot afore eight. Just have a gander at it, the sun's splittin' the chimney-tops – lazy bugger!'

Spud directed his gaze towards the window but could see nothing but a brilliance that pained his eyes. 'Is that ham I smell . . . ?'

'Are you getting up like I asked?' Again she moved laboriously. 'Get a move-on and use the sink, I want tae get some clothes steeped.'

He moved, then paused. His brain seemed to slosh about with an uncontrollable liquidity. The linoleum floor was cold. Unsteadily, he managed the sink. Anguished, the single, brass, swan-necked tap gushed forcefully. The water looked extremely frigid – threatening.

'Stop looking at it as if it was going to eat you,' Beenie frowned.

Plunging his head under the downfall he roared, unable to restrain himself. It served its purpose however, his system was instantly wrenched from its lethargy, adrenalin surged into his blood. He laughed, enjoying the sense of release, and put his arm around her from behind, grasping her milk-firm breast. 'How's about a kiss then?'

'Get off!' she said, pushing his hand away. 'You're no' two minutes wakened.'

'I'm jist right in the mood, I woke up hours ago dyin' for it.'

'If you don't let me get your breakfast oot o' this pan it'll be burned tae a frazzle!' When he persisted she brushed her lips along his cheek. 'There now, give me peace.'

'Is that it?' he asked in the hurt tones of a child.

Beenie glanced at him tiredly. 'Was last night no' enough?'

Spud looked surprised. 'I don't think it could have been. Did I enjoy myself?'

'You want to be on the receiving end one of these times, there's nae living wi' you when you've got a drink in your head.' Instinctively, her hand tested the purple swelling upon her face.

'Whit happened?' he demanded, looking at it with

interest. His protective instincts aroused.

Turning off the heat beneath the pan she stood gazing at the contents, containing her anger. 'Have you no' heard, we had a visit frae the fairies last night, you know, the green people, the wan that did this had tackety boots on!'

'You must have deserved it,' he muttered, recognizing his error, still dull-witted with the drink. Had he remembered doing it he would simply have avoided the subject as they usually did.

'It's over and done with,' she replied indifferently, 'let's just forget it . . . Sit doon.'

'I'll just away for a pee first.' Swiftly he exited out of the front door. She heard him running down the single flight of stairs and banging the door of the stairhead lavatory. Her gaze remained fixed upon vacancy. She was well aware of the ploy. Only a further argument which put her in the wrong would ease his guilt. He wanted to sit down there in the cold cubicle on the landing and return to find his breakfast burned.

Beenie performed a frantic search. Her tranquillizers were gone. 'Damn, blast, and bloody hell!' she uttered, this being the most daring expletive she had ever had the courage to voice.

Spud returned. She now had further ammunition. 'Where are they?'

'Where's whit?'

'You must have moved them,' she ranted. 'God, a house no' the size of a dug kennel and I can never find nothin'!'

His breakfast was on the table. Caught momentarily off-balance he sat down and forked some into his mouth. 'This is – !'

'Where are they!' she demanded loudly.

Deciding, in his weakened condition, to settle for a

draw he continued to chew. He had wished a victory only if it required little effort.

Beenie, however, found herself ill-suited by the silence. Objects, lifted and searched, were returned heavily to their original positions. The atmosphere grew taut.

'You're runnin' about there like a nun in a brothel huntin' for the door!' Spud reacted. 'Whit is it till I get some peace?'

'You know fine well,' she challenged. 'My pills!'

'Did you look in your other pocket?'

Certain of victory she plunged her hand into the folds to prove him wrong. 'How did they manage to get in there?' she asked with genuine surprise, extracting them. Too astonished to register disappointment.

'Two of they things an' you have a struggle tae remember whit time of day it is, much less where you put them!' he frowned. 'Fill up my mug, will you?' He extended the mug in her direction.

Beenie accepted this as it was intended, as a sign that by mutual agreement the intended hostilities could now be satisfactorily brought to a denouement. One pill was the dose, she swallowed two. Each hour having to be clambered through in a body unfit for human habitation, these pills were proving her salvation. She filled his mug. 'You near finished?'

He nodded. 'It was better than it looked.'

'Do us a favour then?'

'Depends?'

'Get out of my sight till these things start workin', I'm fair jumpin' inside?' she spoke with a hint of concern which held a plea for the continuance of the frail bond that existed between them. Minute as it was they had little else . . .

'I'll away doon for the papers.'

She nodded thankfully. 'You'll be goin' for a pint later on, I suppose?'

Surprised, Spud displayed it. 'It's Sunday, I always go tae the club on a Sunday?'

Beenie filled the sink with clothes and then poured in some biological detergent. 'I just want to talk to you beforehand, that's all.'

'Talk away, I'm all ears?' There was caution in his tone.

'Later, we're neither of us in the mood right this minute. It will keep.' With this she made her way laboriously over to the recessed-bed where, with the aid of the brush-pole as an extension of her arm, she made a vain attempt to spread the covers.

'How's about a kiss afore I go?' Despite the truce he felt the need to have her comply.

Her fury was held down by the dull edge of her soreness. Internally she strangled the scream that had been forcing itself upwards. Instead, she spoke with a firm quietude. With what she had to request of him later on she could not afford this anger. 'I'll keep it in mind for when you get back.'

Spud could not see her face but accepted the tone as being promise enough. 'Right, I'll away then.' He exited swiftly.

'And shut the door,' she called. But when she glanced up she saw that, as always, he had left it ajar. The draught of it chilled the room.

Enclosed within the rectangle of worn tenements Hammy and Angus played in the dirt of the back-court. It had not rained for three days but the pitted holes around the back-closes still held large puddles. Nine-year-old Hammy waded through one of their shallows. Angus, who was almost five, circled its perimeters with caution. 'Mammy will murder you,' he warned.

Hammy shrugged, experiencing a glimmering of fear but relishing the emotion and then pretending indifference. 'My shoes will be dry again by the time we go up.' He splashed on, proud of his defiance and chanting:

'Mary had a little lamb,
Her faither shot it deid,
And noo it goes to school wi' her
Between two chunks of breid!'

He felt stronger than all of the world at this moment. Unlimited. Emerging from the water he squelched his shoes pleasantly against the earth.

'Wish I was at school,' Angus bemoaned, knowing that chants such as these were to be learned there.

They sauntered along, bored. With its crumbling brick midden-shelters, each containing three inadequate bins that overflowed, twisted steel clothes-poles, and the remnants of what had once been a line of steel fences separating each allotment, the back-court was too devoid of life to hold any interest for them.

'Look!' Hammy roared with an exaggerated enthusiasm, 'A rainy-beetle!' With a dash he stepped on it, squashed it flat, then spat and intermingled both spit and blood with the point of his shoe. 'Bets it rains afore teatime?' he challenged.

'Is that right, Hammy?' Angus looked upon his brother with respect and awe. 'You know an awfy lot of things!'

Hammy nodded, accepting the statement as the truth he knew it to be. He did know a lot of things. Magic things. There were times when he surprised himself with what he knew.

Spud entered from the opposite side of the enclosure, exiting from the end of a close and making towards the rear of his own. Carefully folded in his pocket were *The News of the World* and *The People*.

'There's Da!' Hammy shouted, exhilarated by this promise of instant relief from the dreadful realms of boredom.

'Hallo you pair, nothin' to do with yourselves?' Spud questioned.

The boys laughed, suddenly alive.

'Lift me under the oxters an gie me a swing?' Hammy begged. Dancing about, unable to be still.

'Get away,' Spud replied. 'You weigh a ton.'

Hammy giggled in disbelief, knowing his father to be capable of anything.

Without a further word, but issuing a relenting sigh, Spud lifted his son under the armpits and began to swing him around. Instantly, the blood rushed to his head. He swayed dizzily, was overwashed by nausea, and was forced to stop.

'That wasnae a real shot?' Hammy groaned.

'Me, me next?' Angus shouted extending his arms.

'Naw,' Spud waved them off. 'I'm no' fit this mornin'. Christ, that nearly did me in.' He breathed heavily. Disappointment filled him, he felt that he had let his son down.

'No' fair,' Angus sulked. 'He always gets everything, he does.'

Spud grinned and nodded. 'Right enough,' he stated proudly, 'but then he's the wan that's goin' to grow up tae be like his faither, right, Hammy?'

'Too true I am, Da!'

Conspiratorially, father and son grinned. This special rapport they accepted as natural to the exclusion of all else, it rendered up a fulfilling warmth.

'I'm telling my mammy if I don't get a swing!' Angus threatened.

They each looked in his direction with something akin to disdain.

'It's a thick ear you'll be gettin',' Spud replied. Then – disruption he did not want – considered what Beenie's response might be, balanced it against the promise of earlier on and drew some soothing coppers from his trouser pocket. 'Here, the pair of you, away and buy yourselves some sweeties.'

'Dead gemmie!' they shouted in ecstatic unison. Hammy, however, was reluctant to forfeit his father's presence for some dubious delight that, now with money safely in hand, could be gleaned at a later date.

'Is it no' right that you earn lots of money, Da?' he prompted.

With a caution inbred of the hunted, Spud paused before answering, 'Well, you know . . . ?'

'I was tellin' my pals!'

'Aw . . .' Spud grinned with some relief. 'I make enough. Aye, don't you fret about that, and I bow to no man for it neither!'

'It's you that tells the daft gaffer an' all the rest o' them what to do, isn't it?'

'If they come tae me for a bit of advice, I give it to them,' Spud replied modestly. 'I mean, education's all right and that, but it canny replace good common sense.'

'Remember when the engineers an' everybody else were lost and you sorted it all oot for them, tell Angus, Da?'

Spud shuffled with embarrassment. 'Jist forget about that, eh . . . ? You go on and on about things like that, them things are jist between you and me, right!'

'Right, Da . . .' Hammy replied, downcast.

They felt awkward with each other, a fractured limb no longer able to transpose this sudden, unwarranted gap.

'We've got a bladder in the close?' Hammy offered.

Spud moved his feet awkwardly against the hard dry earth, torn between his need for stability and silence and the loyalty due to his son. An image of the room and kitchen filled his imagination, Beenie predominant. He experienced a surge of desire that was both deep and demanding and wondered if perhaps she had lied to him about last night.

Witnessing his father's dilemma Hammy further prompted. 'Jist a wee game, jist for a minute . . . ?'

Spud again glanced towards the close and then back to his son. 'Aw right, but jist for a minute mind?'

'I bags being in goal!' Angus chimed.

In anticipation of what was to follow all three of them generated excitement.

'This is the goal,' Angus informed, pointing from one marker against the rear of the building to another.

Hammy returned with the ball. Handing it to his father, giving him the honour of the first kick. 'Bets you canny get it past me?' he taunted, laughing himself at the absurdity of such a statement.

'You're daydreamin'!' Spud retorted playfully. 'When I kick the ball you'll no' even be able to see it!'

'I will,' Angus bobbed in his goalmouth. 'I'll save it.'

All three hesitated, as though by some unconscious command, and breathed deeply. With a flurry, the game began. Spud, swerving exaggeratedly, moved past Hammy and sent the ball, with all his force, soaring between the appointed goalposts. With a loud crack it rebounded off the wall and high into the air. Angus crouched low against the dirt with his hands protectively covering his head.

'Goal . . . !' Spud roared. 'Some goal, eh . . . ? Did you see that goal . . . ? he appealed, then reflectively: 'When I think o' the mugs who are gettin' paid a fortune for the likes o' that. I could beat any wan o' them wi' wan o' my legs sawn off!'

'Again,' Hammy shouted. 'That was a smasher, Da.' Then goadingly lest his father should consider departing, 'Bets you couldnae do it again?'

'Who couldnae . . . ?'

'That was too hard,' Angus complained sullenly. 'It's no' fair when you hit so hard, I'm no' playin' if you do . . .'

After inspecting the pots on her range, Beenie added a pinch of salt to the potatoes. She was brighter, now that the pills had taken their effect. Also there was the unaccustomed solitude – a rarity. Her confidence had expanded. She had already worked out the approach she would adopt with Spud, and was fairly confident of its success.

At that instant Spud entered. 'I'm back, hen!' he shouted unnecessarily. 'I've brought thunder and lightning with me!'

The boys giggled at the suggested notoriety.

She remained with her back to him so that he might not see the anger in her expression. 'You were only supposed to be goin' for a paper and right back?' she accused. His extended absence seemed to belittle her present condition.

'So?'

'Did you have to bring them up wi' you, the dinner's no' near ready?'

'Faither said we could come,' Hammy interjected defensively.

'We were playin' fitba',' Angus informed. 'I was in goal.'

Their voices, usually a pleasure to her, gnawed painfully at her inner ear. She experienced a need to burst into tears or scream or to be excessive in some way in the vague hope that it might serve to relieve this sickening lethargy. She seemed incessantly barbed by emotional and physical harpies.

'Haw, aye, jist wanted me myself, eh . . . ?' Spud grinned, miming the facial signals of a deep sexual rapport that had long since become etiolated.

Beenie turned around, acting out the game, returning the signal. It was one of their many unconsciously agreed rules of equitable survival. 'Aye, jist you.' Her voice was pliable and her smile radiant.

Considering her response over-large Spud sensed danger. Instantly he manufactured a little anger to avoid it. 'You're not on!' he informed her forcefully. 'Whatever it is you're after the answer is no – n.o.'

'I havenae even said yet . . . ?' Beenie smiled, still playing coy.

Spud was definite. 'If you're offerin' that much, that easy, then I canny afford it, it's as simple as that!'

'Jist two lousy pounds!' Beenie rushed out, deciding that only a frontal assault had now any opportunity of success.

'This week?' He was incredulous. 'The now . . . ?'

'This week, every week, a rise? Go on, I know you could manage it if you tried?' She kept her tone low and weak, submissive, then added instinctively, 'One thing about you, you always look after your family, no' like some others I could mention.'

The directness of the request caught him off-balance. He flustered. 'Woman, if I had two quid I'd arrange to have it framed as the eighth wonder o' the world!'

'Mammy,' Hammy intervened, 'can Angus and me have a chocolate biscuit?'

'Your faither an' me's talking,' she snapped, dreading any opportunity for digression.

'Jist wan . . . ?' Hammy moaned, drawing out his voice.

'You,' Beenie glared at him, her husband's favourite. This minor retaliation intimating of others to follow if her ill-favour be gained. Her husband, not the child, the target. 'I'll wring your neck if you don't be quiet!'

Spud received the message. He was reminded of the heights her wrath could attain, and of the thousand deprivations that were hers to inflict. 'It's jist not possible,' he pleaded, but recognized doubt in his own voice. 'You'll jist have to cut down on other things.'

'Where? I've got two boys to buy clothes for?' She sensed victory.

'They get new clothes nearly every week, woman, they're ruined!'

'Aye, and they're goin' to stay that way. What we didnae have they're goin' to get. My weans arenae goin' to go through what the likes of us went through. Are you goin' to start denyin' your ain family for the sake of a few extra pints? Naw, no' you, I don't believe it!'

All three faces were now trained upon him, attempting to determine his response to this accusation. Confronted by them he realized that he, if his present position was to be maintained, had no other option but to relent. The present housekeeping money he did give her was more than sufficient, almost one-and-a-half times what his mates gave their wives, but he could afford another two. In fact, he would profit from it. Until now he had been avoiding Sunday work, unable to commit himself either way.

Actually he was pleased now that the decision had been taken for him.

'There's some Sunday work goin',' he said, maintaining his voice at the crushed level of martyrdom. 'I'll still have Saturday afternoon off.' Internally he felt it to be something of a victory. His own folding money would be increased considerably and he had, to all appearances, openly immolated himself. Beenie was frowning; before the children she had deprived him of his only day off. Spud waved away all protestations before any were attempted. 'My decision, my choice!'

Beenie, aware that if she had considered the possibility of Sunday work she could have asked for as much as five pounds and in all probability gained it, was now forced to accept what she had requested. The confrontation, however, was over. A seasoned campaigner, she accepted defeat, assured of future victories. 'You're jist a big darlin'!' she exclaimed, actually quite proud of him for having emerged the victor, and kissed him on the cheek with genuine warmth. Each unsure of what the other was intimating (since the initial action had been entirely spontaneous), they were reluctant to offer less themselves in case it should be accepted as a slight and encourage hostility. Their arms encircled each other with cautious enthusiasm.

'Two fatty bellies!' Hammy laughed as he witnessed their awkwardness, protruding his own stomach to match.

Spud, over-conscious of his beer belly, broke off, hesitated, then initiated a game by grasping at his son's stomach. 'No' as fat as yours, let me feel?'

Delighted, Hammy feigned resentment. 'Get away!' he giggled, bumping against the table. Spud followed, upsetting one of the light chairs in his eagerness. Beenie allowed it to continue for as long as she could bear. Each additional collision and squeal sent an ever-enlarging shock-wave resounding harshly against the raw inner dome of her cranium. Allowing for its present fragility she felt that it was about to rend and permit her vacillating brain to explode free and tear the life from her.

'Enough!' she screamed, only seconds later recognizing the voice as her own. She had not wanted to scream and regretted the antagonism it might allow.

They paused. Then stopped. 'His fault,' Spud said brightly, panting to regain his breath. 'Cheeky wee sod.'

'Your fault!' Hammy challenged, wishing to continue.

'Jist you dare . . . !' his mother warned. Extracting a pound note from her purse she handed it to her husband. 'Here, since the pair o' you have that much spare energy then yous can run back down the stairs and fetch me a wee bag o' coal.'

'Ach, Beenie . . .' Spud groaned, 'I've only jist come up?'

'A cup o' tea will be waiting by the time you get back,' Beenie stated, no longer listening.

Resigned, Spud turned to Hammy. 'Right then, it's a race, you and me!' And with this he went off through the door with a clear advantage.

Hammy squealed and then followed, leaving a vacuum.

Once again the room became a haven. Clearly not wishing to be disturbed, Angus was squatted in the corner, silently at play. Beenie glanced. She had a fear of late and it now nagged at her. She found herself inadvertently antagonizing him. As now, at peace, she could not restrain herself from entering his private sphere in the hope of reclaiming him into her own.

'Whit's the notion of playin' way across there?' she asked cheerfully.

He did not reply. She returned to her chores, wanting to leave him alone. Inventing self-occupying tasks. She rubbed at the furniture and dusted the mantelpiece unnecessarily.

'Did you no' hear?' she insisted, damning herself for having done so.

'Playin',' he replied, quietly, reluctantly.

She attempted gaiety. 'Did you say playin', playin' at what . . . ?'

'Playin',' he answered sullenly. A deliberate, quite unmistakable rebuff.

Suddenly, blindly, irrationally, she experienced the impulse physically to injure him in retaliation for the pain he was inflicting in depriving her of his immediate love. The guilt following this awful reaction only suffused her with an even greater passion. Her need of his love and good opinion was insistent to the exclusion of all else. Each instant she found it necessary to fight to contain herself, to remain an adult for fear of frightening him by rushing to overwhelm him with unrestrained passion.

'You always used to sit on my knee when naebody else was in?' she accused.

He refused to reply. She ventured tentatively. 'Is it because you don't like me any more?' The question was stupid to a child, she realized it. Yet, paradoxically, felt that this alone might be the one concrete truth. In her present condition she felt incapable of being truly loved. Undeserving. A biological monstrosity. She fully realized that others had no way of feeling the vibrant glow of internal life that served to sustain her.

He whispered something.

'Whit?' she rushed out in desperation.

'Nothin' . . .'

'Come on, whit was it you said?'

'Fatty belly,' he whispered.

'Still canny hear you?' she said, inching hopefully closer.

For an instant he remained silent. Then spat out, 'Big, horrible fatty-belly!'

She was astounded. 'Whit?'

'Are so . . .' he replied unrelentingly. 'No' play boxin'.'

Beenie recalled the incident. 'But I canny let you hit my stomach now – ?' she began, then realized that there was nothing further to be said. The extent of her quandary was revealed to her. She did, instinctively, shy away from his excessive approaches, fearing the damage he might inflict.

There could now only be compromise, never again the fine intimacy they had known. The awful sadness of it sank heavily further to repress her spirit. What she found so dreadful was the lack of choice. She was committed, maternally, biologically, instinctively, always to the weakest and least defensible.

The atmosphere was shattered as Spud burst in through the doorway shouldering a small paper-wrapped bag of coal. Triumphant in exhaustion he shouted, 'I won, it's me the winner!'

'Second!' Hammy acclaimed. They stood, breathing heavily, as if awaiting their deserved applause.

'Get your hands washed the pair of you!' Beenie said brusquely.

They giggled, conspiratorial in their obedience, and went directly to the sink. Too content to have offered objection and invited disruption. Playfully each flicked fingertips of water into the other's eyes.

Beenie's features darkened physically under the strain. She poured the tea and placed out some chocolate biscuits – a full dozen, they vanished almost instantly. Their three brown-rimmed mouths and voraciously munching lips pained her vision – it seemed akin to a physical assault directed explicitly in her direction.

'I've heard o' greed – !' she wailed, agonized that they should inflict this upon her. 'But you three!'

Spud, considering it more than his due that in respect to his previous generosity he be allowed to reign supreme for the remainder of the day, pointed a finger so that she might be in no doubt as to whom he was addressing. 'Just you keep your mouth shut, that's whit they were there for – eatin'!'

The inevitable hiatus between peace and discord. A mutual dreading of what seemed to be the inevitable. All four paused. Prisoners of all of the previous altercations that served so firmly to predict and direct their responses.

Almost unconsciously Beenie went through the motions of sweeping the floor. When she finally did look up into their expectant faces she said, 'I could fairly do wi' a new pair of curtains, them up there are a right mess.' Her tone was blank.

In confusion the boys and their father collapsed into a wary silence.

'Mrs White had a fright
In the middle o' the night,
She saw a ghost eatin' toast
Half-way up a lamp-post!' Hammy chanted.

Angus, once again bored, wandered by his side around the dullness of the back-court.

'Can I go and look in the middens for lucky things?' Angus begged.

'Naw!'

'Aw, how no' . . . ?'

''Cause you'll get manky and I'll get belted for it!'

'Can I play wi' your motor now that it's broke?'

'Naw!'

'How no', it's no' worth anything noo?'

'Jist because.'

Sunday was a terrible day for them. It lacked the interest of a weekday and the excitement of a Saturday. It was a nothing day.

'Where does the dark go when the sun comes oot, Hammy?'

'Dae you never stop askin' daft questions?' Hammy retorted. 'You don't hear big folk askin' questions all the time, dae you?'

'Naw . . .'

'Well then . . .'

They had been wandering around this tight circle for more than two hours; with each step it seemed to grow oppressively smaller.

'Hallo, hen!' Grinning euphorically, Spud entered the kitchen.

Beenie glanced up with feigned amazement. 'They're no' shutting for half an hour yet, whit happened, was there a fire?'

'I've had enough to be goin' on with.'

'That's as plain as day.'

'Besides,' he added, altering his tone to that of muted sex, 'I had more important things on my mind when I left.'

Stronger again, due to her pills, Beenie replied, 'If it's the same things as are glintin' in your eyes then you can forget them!'

'Aw, come on, dae I no' get a wee thank you for the extra two quid?'

'Aye, well, there is that of course,' she replied, acknowledging the debt. 'See me round about bedtime.'

'I'd blow up and burst afore then,' he laughed, his confidence growing.

Hammy rushed in through the front door. 'Is my Da back frae the pub yet?' he shouted breathlessly. Halting abruptly at the sight of Spud. 'Hallo, Da?'

'Away out again, Hammy,' Spud pleaded. 'Your mother an' me are busy right now!'

Evasively, Beenie turned her attentions towards the boy. 'You've no' gone and left that wean oot there by himself?'

'He's aw right,' Hammy replied, his voice lacking assurance.

'You've better no' be lying tae me?' she stated fearfully. 'The streets these days, if the weans arenae bein' knocked doon they're being abused by some mental pervert!'

'Somebody's watchin' him,' Hammy lied.

'Never mind that, Beenie. Send the boy out an' let's you and me talk nice . . . ?'

Unable to deflect herself from the pull of this flattery Beenie softened. Her dissident body opposed her mind's urge to be desired. 'You and your talk,' she replied lightly, 'jist look where it got me?' She looked at him, wanting to see in him a paramour. A hint of promise. A lover. Anything. But he was drunk and she realized that she would be unable to face the sweaty struggle that the reality of it would prove to be.

'I don't remember you complainin' at the time?' Spud grinned – a memory of heat.

She nodded, accepting this. 'I was three-quarters way full o' vodka and lime and bein' lifted as near as I'll ever get tae heaven on this earth after havin' spent the entire day ower stove and sink. Who's capable o' thought at a time like that . . .?' She frowned. 'Jist once I'd like tae have one that was planned aforehand.'

'Da . . . ?' Hammy insisted, reminding them of his presence.

'Will you stop pesterin' me and away oot!' Spud snapped.

Welcoming the intervention Beenie came to her son's aid. 'He's been standin' there like a wee martyr, it's only right you should see whit he wants.'

Hammy proffered a toy motor car with a twisted wheel. 'Can you fix it, I said you could fix it, it's only a wee bit broke?'

Spud glanced at it. 'Nae bother, two seconds!' He was genuinely pleased at the apparent brevity of the task. 'Now right oot again when it's finished.'

'Dead gemmie,' Hammy danced. 'I told them you could, I told them you could fix anythin'!'

Spud went to his box and unsteadily retrieved his pliers while Beenie, moving adroitly around him, lifted a basin full of wrung-out clothes. 'I'll away doon the back and hang these out. I don't suppose any o' you two are goin' to put yourselves out o' joint offerin' to give a hand?' No reply was forthcoming, she had not expected any. Directly to Spud she said, 'And jist you mind you don't go and break that thing allthegither, the state you're in!' With that she left.

'You'll no' break it, will you, Da?' Hammy questioned fearfully, having already noted his father's condition.

Spud considered himself above reply. 'You brought it tae the right man!' he said, as if to himself, and listening to his own voice reassuringly.

'I told them that!' Hammy informed with pride.

'Aye, who . . . ?'

'Every one o' my pals, especially Tattie!'

'Tattie McFee, Geordie McFee's boy?'

'He's my bestest pal.'

Spud looked disgruntled. 'Canny say I think aw that much o' his faither – a right big blaw. Good for pushin' people aboot jist because he used tae be a bit o' a boxer!'

'It's Tattie's motor, we swapped.'

The wheel refused to straighten, first bending too extreme in one direction and then in the other. 'Was it broken when you swapped?'

'Same as now.'

'That's my boy,' Spud sang gleefully, 'sharp as the November wind. Sure I'll fix it for him, why no'? Bet that faither o' his couldnae, big animal that he is.' With revitalized enthusiasm he once again bent to the task. 'Come on . . .' he grinned, ceasing momentarily as a further thought struck him. He looked up. 'Let's have a gander at whit you wangled out o' him?'

Proudly, and with an adequate amount of flourish, Hammy produced his prize. It was a Joan the Wad charm piece. 'I've been tryin' tae get it aff him for ages,' he enthused. 'It's a magic thing, it works and all, I've seen it, Tattie finds things all the time.'

'You've been had!' Spud retorted angrily. 'Taken tae the cleaners.'

'Naw, Da?' Hammy replied with astonishment.

Spud's features darkened with thought. 'Did that yin threaten you and make you swap?'

'He's my bestest pal, Da. He only gave it me because o' that. Everybody's wanted it for ages.'

'I'm no' havin' you being' scared o' him nor naebody else, dae you hear me? I'm no' havin' nae mammy's boy in my family. You should have stood up tae him and fought back like you know I would have done!'

'But I'm a good fighter, Da. I can beat Tattie . . .!'

'Nae need tae make it worse by tellin' lies, I'm no'

havin' nae boy o' mine makin' a fool of himself in front o' the entire street.' Frustratedly he tugged at the pliers. The plastic shell of the car was already cracking under the strain.

Before such unwarranted suggestions, Hammy experienced a sense of utter bewilderment. Cautious of his father's mounting fury he attempted to further explain. 'But it's no' like that . . . ?'

'Dae you think I don't know these people?' He glared, then, after thinking, dropped his tone to the level of a friendly conspirator. 'Look, tell you whit, run doon and give him that stupid thing back. Jist tell him the motor is broken and the deal is off, how's that . . . ?'

Awestruck by such dishonesty Hammy faltered. 'We wet thumbs and palmed on it, Da? Nae turn-roons, nae changey-backs. I don't want tae anyway, I've always wanted this thing, it's smashin' so it is!'

'You're scared!' Spud accused, 'Yella. I'm no' havin' nae cowards in this family; we might be a lot o' things but we've nane o' us ever been guilty o' that!' Having momentarily forgotten the fragility of the task he compressed the pliers and the toy split from end to end with a loud crack! 'Noo look whit you've gone and made me dae!'

'It's broke!'

' 'Course it's broke, whit else did you expect, pesterin' me while I was workin' on it?'

'You broke it . . . ?'

'Never mind,' Spud consoled, considering that the matter had now settled itself. 'I'll buy you another wan – two if you like. There, how's that – two motors?'

'It wasnae mine, it was Tattie's!' Only his astonishment served to restrain his tears.

'Don't you go startin' that again,' Spud warned. 'The

motor is yours, and that daft wee lassie's doll is his. Now forget it, I'm no' askin' any more, I'm tellin' that's an end to it!'

They existed now in a realm previously unknown to them, from lack of experience their emotions floundered hopelessly. Each wishing for some timely intervention which might somehow and miraculously undo all that had gone immediately before. They viewed each other strangely. Sudden strangers and appalled by their own sense of deprivation.

Thankfully, Beenie arrived. Herself an animal raised within a confined and therefore hostile environment, her keen senses caught the situation instantaneously. 'You could cut this atmosphere wi' a knife?' she commented.

'It's this boy!' Spud volunteered. 'I'm right fed up wi' the very sight o' him!'

Beenie directed her eyes towards the ceiling. 'Five minutes I've been away.' Her gaze lowered and fell upon the broken toy. 'You've no' gone and broke the wean's motor?'

'It was Tattie's . . .' Hammy said, allowing his tears to flow.

'He wants tae play wi' dolls noo!'

Habitually, Beenie closed the argument out of her mind. In order to survive she contended only with the untrivial ones. She directed herself to Hammy. 'Away doon and fetch the wean up, the dinner's near ready.' Hammy shuffled uncomfortably. 'Don't jist stand there, go and get him?'

'He ran away frae me,' Hammy confessed, ''cause I wouldnae let him play wi' me and my pals.'

'He did whit!'

'I tried tae catch him,' Hammy explained fearfully, 'but he was too fast.'

'I'll murder him, the wee bissim!' Beenie exclaimed. 'Aw this time, anythin' could be happening tae him, he could be gettin' his throat cut, or even worse.' She turned to Spud for comfort but he was, from lack of sustenance, beginning to nod off. 'Trust a man,' she roared indignantly. 'Your youngest could be lyin' in the street wi' nae heid on his shoulders!' She went on a frantic search for her pills. 'You, Hammy, you get yourself doon them stairs an' don't you dare show your face through that door again withoot him!' She glanced towards the stove. 'If that dinner gets ruined I'll make a hole in the Clyde with the lot of yous!'

The kitchen door burst open.

'I've got him, Ma!' Hammy shouted, dragging a reluctant, kicking Angus in behind him.

'You're nothin' but a big, snottery-nosed sneak!' Angus screamed.

Beenie erupted, unable to restrain herself despite the pills. 'Bad wee bugger! Have you any notion o' whit you've been puttin' me through?'

'I was only hiding doon the close,' Angus explained, hopeful of avoiding punishment, and now over-eager to converse with her.

'Near aff my heid, I was!' Beenie flyted. Her hand flew out and connected with the side of his face. He went tottering across and then down on to the floor. 'Get up!' she demanded, feeling that her rage would only be diminished in the act of knocking him down once again.

'That was sore,' Angus pouted.

The childishness of his expression touched her maternal instincts and she limited herself to a further verbal assault. 'If your faither wasnae sleepin', I'd batter the living daylights out o' you!'

'Who the hell can sleep wi' this racket goin' on?' Spud asked, disgruntled.

'You!' Beenie turned upon him. 'Some faither . . . that wean could have been in hospital fightin' for his very breath and all you can do is sleep!'

Not yet fully released from sleep Spud ignored the challenge. 'Whit's that terrible smell . . . ?'

'That,' Beenie ranted, 'is whit's left o' the dinner I spent hours makin'! You two,' she turned upon the children, 'get into that room till you're shouted, and you,' she turned to Spud, 'jist let me hear wan word out o' you aboot your belly rumblin' and I'll stick a knife in it!'

In the face of her awful wrath they obeyed. Deriving energy from her anger Beenie set about preparing yet another meal.

In the darkness of the late-night room Angus lay awakened listening to the voices of his parents in the kitchen. He could see coloured pictures whenever he closed his eyes. Superman in light blue and red, Spiderman casting dark webs. Images from the colour telly. Hammy was awake. Even through the blackness he could sense it.

'Hammy?' he whispered. There was no reply. He tried again. 'Hammy . . . ?'

'Whit?'

'Are you wakened?'

'Naw, I'm sleepin', leave me be.' There was a certain sadness to his tone.

'Can you no' waken up for a wee minute and talk tae me?'

'Naw!'

The reply was firm.

In the kitchen Beenie hauled herself from her chair and

switched off the television before the broadcasting company could coerce her into being assaulted by their nightly rendering of 'God Save the Queen'.

'Dae they do that on purpose, do you think?'

'Whit?'

'Make the adverts better than the programmes?'

Spud, heavy from the want of sleep, did not reply.

'The weans enjoyed the space monster picture earlier on,' she continued. 'Big saft nellie that you are, buyin' them all o' them sweeties, you near made the two o' them sick.'

'Ach, they deserved it, Sunday's a lousy day at the best o' times,' he yawned. 'Here, whit was the matter wi' oor Hammy?'

'Nothin',' Beenie frowned. 'He jist fell aff his rocky-horse for the first time and discovered that the ground is hard.'

'Whit rocky-horse . . . ?'

Beenie nodded, unheeding. 'Fancy a cup o' tea?'

'Whit I want doesnae come out o' teapots.'

'We'll have tea.' She filled the kettle.

Angus, having remained silent for as long as possible, whispered, 'Hammy?'

'I'm goin' tae throttle you in a minute,' Hammy menaced in the dark.

'I want tae ask you somethin'?'

'I don't know nothin'!'

'It's jist a wee thing?' Angus pleaded. 'It's no' even the size o' nothin'?'

'Aw right then, whit is it?'

'How's it no' rainin' yet, Hammy . . . ?'

'How should I know?'

'You said it would?'

'Ach, that . . .'

'Did you no' dae it right, is it no' goin' tae rain now?'

'Naw . . . noo get tae sleep.'

'But how no', Hammy?'

'Jist because, that's aw . . .'

They listened, each to the breathing of the other.

'Were you only kidding me?' Angus questioned.

Hammy nodded unseen. 'Dae you think I'm simple enough tae believe in daft things the likes o' that? Noo let me get some sleep, I've got school tae go to in the mornin'.'

In the pitch they hearkened to breathing and the muted whisperings from through the wall.

'Come on,' Spud frowned, afraid of falling asleep before his request had been fulfilled. 'Let's get tae bed?'

'Is that all you ever think o'?' Beenie asked, clearing the dishes.

'I've had my drink and I've had my telly, whit else is there?'

She nodded philosophically. 'You go on, I'll jist wash through their socks and underpants then I'll be right with you?'

'You'll come now, you're no' goin' to be up half the night?'

'I'll be there, jist you go on in and get the bed warm.'

Lacking sufficient energy to do otherwise, Spud complied.

Soon he was asleep. Beenie, by the sink, listened to his snores and heard them as the most pleasant sound of her day. With a grunt his body rolled over, his snores subsided, and he dreamed.

She paused,
halting her actions
so that
there might be
Silence . . .

WHO WANTS THE TWENTIETH CENTURY ANYWAY?

OSWALD WYND

WHEN I say I'm an Aberdeen Jew everyone shouts with laughter; but the fact is there are quite a few of us making money up amongst the Scots. My grandfather started with a furniture store which has now become an antique business, that's progress for you. And I know more about Sheraton than half the experts at a London auction where the most impressive characters . . . with beards no Yiddisher would dare wear . . . can still be taken in by a carefully contrived fake. I stopped a man paying seven thousand pounds for a commode that was a kind of Irish stew cunningly put together, most of the bits junk, and what thanks do I get? Does the auctioneer love me? Does any dealers' syndicate want to cut me in? It's hard to be an honest man in this business.

Americans come all the way up to my showrooms in Union Street dressed like Eskimos against our good old Scottish climate, and I go all over the world looking for little surprises to have waiting for them. It puts a lot of travel against business expense and that's the only way to get around these days. I like travel and it's funny that

I had never got out to see my sister before, but perhaps that's mainly because down where she lives, in the sun, there aren't many antiques that you can buy. I was going to have a hard job getting this trip past my tax consultant because none of the specimens of native art I brought back are going to impress anyone much. I can maybe sell the little stinkwood carved heads for twenty pounds apiece, but not to the kind of Americans who fly up to me. These are mostly well-preserved girls in their fifties wearing Tokyo pearls set in Holland and some of them with husbands who are more easily transportable than poodles.

My sister married Sammy Leibnitz who was a rich man when she married him and has got richer since. He sells cars, and though he says the business is ruined these days in one week while I am there he gets rid of two Mercedes and a Jag, which is the kind of ruin where you still eat and drink. They have a lovely home, a ranch type to which they added more rooms for new Leibnitzes, built in a kind of U shape around the sort of blue-tinted swimming pool that would make a Californian feel at home.

Rachel I wondered about a little before I went out, because Mama got a bit plump on kosher Aberdeen kippers and such foods, and my sister was very like her in many ways, a home girl, and all for the family. But after seven years Rachel was still as thin as a pole from living on meat cooked in the garden and no starches. She still had very good looks and all her own teeth, and welcomed little brother with floods of heartwarming tears. For the first three days she talked about the good life out there, not much anti-Semitism because the whole economy would collapse if that ever got going. Sammy wasn't really fat either; his old man had gone that way and had a terminal coronary and Sammy had always kept that in mind, like a good husband should when the potatoes are passed.

They entertain a lot. Somebody rings up and says can they come round and you say yes and ring twenty more people. All the best parties grow like this and they have a lot of top-level parties. The climate helps, too. You flow out of the house into the garden after the native boy has gone around with a squirt gun getting rid of mosquitoes in the living area. I still got a lot of bites but I was much more uncomfortable on this score in Western Australia where the mosquitoes are six inches long.

Rachel was full of cute hostess tricks. She got tired of hanging out Japanese paper lanterns round the garden on short notice so she got Sammy to import her a few authentic stone ones from Tokyo at a price he told me all about as he touched one of them. But the effect was good. You pulled a switch on the porch and the garden glowed and even the people who had seen those lanterns seventeen times already that year made noises of delight and said Rachel was so clever. It's not so hard to be when you've married a Sammy. They even had floodlighting on a special tree which sends out fat red flowers on totally nude branches so it looks a bit like a fan dancer before the music warms up. A really nice home.

As a furniture dealer, though, there wasn't anything I'd shout over in the contents. In the bedrooms everything was fitted, and that was fine, including camphor-wood cupboards, but in the living area you stood amongst all Rachel's homey clutter and decided the garden was better. I nearly brought her out a small piece of Buhl that I'd found hard to sell for the right price but was glad I'd decided not to. It wouldn't have gone well with a chromium lamp standard growing straight out of a wicker-covered table with metal legs. That kind of thing really hurts me so I lived in the garden practically all the time I was there.

You could, too, it never rained. They'd had rain three months before and were expecting it again, and several times it clouded up, but then the clouds just evaporated. I don't know where they got the water from but the arrangements must have been good, for the sprinklers went all the time, and what with two native boys for the weeding the groomed look was almost embarrassing. There was no place you could throw a bottle cap.

At night it was beautiful, the tropic stars not crowded out by those lanterns, and you were conscious all the time of an arc of sky like an astrodome right over your head. I drank too much and relaxed and ate more barbecued meat than I'd ever seen in my whole life. You could even have it for breakfast if you wanted to. The vitality all around was something to see. Nobody ever got tired and the men in their late fifties were still just boys with a new sports car.

I never saw any poverty, at least not close. Maybe they drove me through it fast. I did notice natives lying around asleep a lot and once I asked Rachel what they ate. She said: 'What? Oh, a kind of porridge, I think. Made from mealies.' There are some high-pressure US executives operating factories in Scotland who say that porridge makes the natives sleepy with us, too, but I think this is a biased viewpoint. In Aberdeen they drinky whisky and are not sleepy at all. Ask anyone who has tried to buy an Angus bull at an economy price.

Two days before I flew home there was a bigger party than usual. Three people phoned up and Rachel phoned about thirty-five more. She came into the room where I was getting into tropic-weight trousers wearing a white dress that could have been sent to her straight from Dior in return for her measurements.

'Oh, sorry,' she said.

'It's only little brother, remember? What's the matter?'

'It's Ruby. You met her. The old girl whose mouth always stays open except when there's food in it. She's early. She always is. Go out and give her your charm, Jon. I've got things to see to.'

I put on my jacket. You wear your jacket for the first half hour and if the party's a flop you keep it on. I went out into the lantern-lit night and found Ruby filling the whole of a rather spacious iron chair which had been imported from Harrods in London. The old girl already had her first drink, from the native boy in attendance, and I was provided for at once, too.

'Well,' said Ruby. 'Here I am first again.'

'Someone's got to be. It's a pleasure to see you.'

'Don't use your European manners on me, young man. I'm too old and fat to be worth them. Sarah tells me you're not married. Why?'

'We're careful in my family. It's got to be love *and* an expansion of the business. That takes some searching for.'

'Don't let your hair fall out while you're looking. Sit down. Haven't you met any pretty girls here who would bring you out to the only sensible place left to live in?'

'I've seen a lot of pretty girls. They're all pretty in this country.'

'I never was. Look at me. At twenty-five I weighed a lot already. But I've been a good wife. Ask Abel.'

'I'll remember to. Where is your husband?'

'Oh, business. He gets home later. And am I expected to wait around? No, I'll say that. He doesn't expect me to wait around. When I give a party he isn't there, but he comes in later. Still, do I complain? I say every two years: "Abel, you got to take me to Europe again." So he does. We go to France. I like France. Maybe it's the food you get. In the heat you can cook and cook but it never tastes the same. Oh, I'm born and bred in this country but there are things you don't get. I admit that. But we've got everything else. Don't you think so?'

'It's certainly quite a place to live. At this level.'

'What do you mean "at this level", eh? You think we got a lot of poor whites we hide some place? I tell you, you won't find no poor whites. Not a one. Even if you're lazy you're not poor. Not like Europe. The new ones come out here and they get a native maid two days after they land. Maybe their husband is only a mechanic but they get them a native girl. Before a house sometimes. We get a lot of immigrants every year from Britain and what do they look like after six weeks? They got a tan and a fixed smile. That's the kind of country this is.'

I didn't say anything. When I first arrived I had a few questions and I asked some of them. What I got was a record. They could all put on the same record. After a while you didn't want to hear it. They were just sounds on plastic all ready and waiting. All they did was lower the needle.

Ruby lowered the needle.

'The things people say. It's because they don't know the country. Have they ever come out here to see for themselves? Oh, no. We oppress the natives. You know this, you won't get better-fed, happier natives anywhere. And that's a fact. Nowhere. You go and look. You go to one of those new free black countries. Look at those natives. So they've got freedom? I'll tell you what they've got. They've got to bow down to a black man, that's what they've got to do. And it's not natural for them.'

'You mean they ought to have a white man to bow down to?'

Ruby sat up.

'Well, now, who's twisting things, eh ? You don't sound like Rachel's brother at all when you say things like that. What's wrong with the hospitality you've had out here ?'

'It's been wonderful.'

'So you go back with the ideas you brought in, is that it ? To tell them what's wrong with us ?'

'I'm not going to tell them anything. All I've seen is this.'

'What's wrong with this ?' Ruby snapped. 'You see that native boy over there ? You see a man that brought you a glass of liquor just now ? What's he ? A servant, you think. I'll tell you something. That servant is better off than a million natives somewhere else. Don't you see him smiling all day ? When he brings you things ? Don't you see him smiling ?'

'Yes,' I said, wishing more people would come.

'Nobody ever says it. That we like the natives. That's what they never say. I've had the same cook for twenty-three years. Twenty-three years, that's how long I've had her. You should hear my cook talking about natives who get too big for their hats. She can tell you. It's just the same in business. My husband has two hundred natives in his factory. He built houses for them. You hear people saying that we make the natives live away from their husbands or wives. Well, that's only in special cases sometimes. My husband built those houses. They've got water in them and everything. He pays his men more than the rate around here. You know this, he's like a father to his natives. Oh, I'm not saying he doesn't get a bad one sometimes. But Abel knows what to do with a bad native. A rotten apple in the barrel, he says. So he throws it out. Abel is a firm man, but a just one and the native knows that. He never has any trouble in his factory.'

Ruby took a long drink but it didn't stop her for more than quarter of a minute.

'You get hooligans everywhere, don't you? Look at London. You read about plenty of hooligans in London these days. Boys and girls still, going off on motor bikes and smashing up a town. And football matches. People get killed at football matches. That happens in good old England. And Belfast. What you got to say about Belfast, eh?'

'Nothing.'

Ruby took a cigarette from me.

'I'm not saying we don't have trouble sometimes. We've got hooligans here, too. Natives too big for their hats, that's what they are. And a lot of bad natives come into this country from outside. That's something we've got to stop. Our own natives would be all right if they just got left alone. And don't say we're not educating them, either. Because we are.'

'How many native doctors have you got?'

'What?' Ruby sat up straight. 'So you do ask questions, eh? Well, maybe I can't answer that one, but Abel will. He'll be here later. But I know we've got plenty native doctors. For their people. And lawyers and all that. You ask Abel for figures. He's got everything off. I'll tell him to tell you what you want to know.'

'Well, Ruby . . . !' said Sammy, coming over looking hot in his jacket.

'We've got an investigator here,' Ruby said. 'Somebody out checking up on us.'

'You mean Jon? Why now, Jon never investigated anything but a piece of furniture in his life.'

'Thanks,' I said.

'He thinks we're just using the natives.'

Sammy went solemn.

'Well, in a kind of way you could say we are. But we're thinking about them, too. All we need is some time to get things sorted out.'

He saw our glasses were empty and turned to call the native who was coming down the steps with a laden tray. Rachel came down them, too, with four people, and three more behind. The party had started. They took Ruby off my hands.

It was a good party. Half the people there wouldn't be seeing me again before I went home and they made it sound as though this fact hurt them. I was told that I ought to sell up in Aberdeen or whatever outlandish place I lived and come out here and build a nice house to be near Rachel, seeing that neither of us had any family left but each other. It wouldn't be hard, they said, to get a girl to put in that house. Did I fancy anyone around tonight?

Nice people in a nice garden on a beautiful evening and later on we sang and I got to thinking about how I would remember this always, and Rachel in her home with everything she could want and Sammy's strong, comforting voice as background. She was a lucky girl all right. I knew how cold I was going to find my granite house in Aberdeen after this, and how restrained I'd find my housekeeper's greeting when I got back to it. Mrs Macpherson is a good housekeeper but she prefers to look after me alone. People are not supposed to drop in, she likes plenty of warning so that she can see the silver is polished and, naturally, I have quite a bit of silver so that entertaining is something of a problem, mostly I meet people in restaurants. Still, it's my father's and Mama's house, and I've got a feeling for that. I also like my garden which I do myself and each year going out to see if the roses have really survived the blasting of the

January gales. Every piece of furniture inside is something I just couldn't sell. If I brought some of those things out here they'd probably fall apart in the heat or the ants would get them. Funny the little things that keep you where you are, when the problem isn't money. I suppose I could sell up now and go into business with Sammy. It might be interesting to deal in something as perishable as a motor car for a change.

'We're going to miss you, boy,' Sammy said from his chair alongside, as though he was psychic.

'Thanks.'

'Well, you fit in. You really do. It's done Rachel a power of good having you. I keep telling her she ought to go to the old country for a visit, but she won't leave the kids with me and the servants. She's that kind of a girl. Maybe later on when they're a bit bigger we'll bring the whole batch over. Though that would bankrupt me, I'm telling you. You know, kids get more expensive every year.'

'So my friends tell me.'

'It's time you did something about it, Jon. A man in a big house by himself. It's not right.'

'I'm away half the time.'

'Even then. You like it here, Jon?'

'Who wouldn't?'

'Well, if that's the way you feel why not come out, like everyone's saying? This is the good life, boy. Show me where you can get a better.'

'I don't think I could.'

'Then where's the argument for Aberdeen?' Sammy asked.

I couldn't give him an answer, even with the obvious one that I liked what I was doing and it wouldn't be easy to go on doing that in a country where most people seemed to prefer their lamps growing out of tables on poles. Or went all modern Swedish.

The native boy brought us more drinks. He was smiling. Maybe he'd had a few himself.

I looked around at all those women who had never in their lives done a week's wash, even at an automatic machine. They didn't cook, most of them, and none polished, meeting in each other's houses to pass the mornings away. They all looked happy on it, too, as if it was a good thing to have a hard-working husband while you could put your feet up whenever you wanted. Even children weren't a great problem. You just stretched the household budget a little and brought in another native girl. Little things like this kept the years at bay, too. You couldn't tell whether a lot of these women were in their thirties or forties and the older ones made a point of their years with the lavender hair that goes so well with pearls. Certainly the light in the garden now was gentle, but I'd seen them all in the day, too. They were always smiling, like the natives. When hubby came home it was drinks time while the cook sang a native song as she basted the joint.

All the men had their jackets off now. It was a good party.

I'd run out of cigarettes and went into the house to get some more. Rachel was in the living-room. She was standing by the phone. I'd never seen her looking like that before. She's only five years older than I am, but right then she looked like someone who'd had fifteen years of her life plucked away. She had a hand down to lean on the table. Her face, under its tan, had gone a kind of brown-grey.

'What is it?'

She just shook her head.

'Rachel! What the hell's happened?'

'It's . . . the police.' She couldn't get the right pitch into her voice. 'The police just phoned.'

'About what?'

'I . . . I can't tell her!'

I went over. I put my hands on her shoulders.

'You can tell me.'

She put a head forward against the front of my shirt.

'Oh, God! Oh, God in Heaven.'

'Rachel!'

'It's Abel. He came home late. To the house. On the stoep . . . He was putting his key in the door, they think. His key in the door . . .'

'Then what?'

'He was killed. With an axe. They . . . found the axe.'

I took a deep breath. It made her lift her head. I saw into her eyes. I saw terror.

'They think it was one of his native workers. He . . . he fired one.'

One word came into my mind. It sat there. It was 'hooligan'.

'Oh, Jon! I get so frightened. For myself. For the children. For Sammy. I don't know . . . Is it the Yiddish fear, Jon? Of the place you're in turning against you? Is it that? It is that, Jon?'

I couldn't tell her. I just held my sister in my arms for the sobs that shook her, and from her me.

'We'll have to . . . Ruby!'

'Yes,' I said. 'You want me to go out and bring her in?'

'Would you? I'll get a room ready. I'll . . .'

She looked at me again. Then she swung away to a mirror, looking at her own face.

It was one of the most terrible things I've ever had to do, that going out for Ruby and bringing the old girl in as she kept shouting she knew it was Abel phoning like he usually did to say he was tired and wouldn't be around to the party. Rachel was waiting for us, her face still with that strange colour under sunburn, but that was all. She wasn't crying any more for herself, for her children, or for the place in which she lived.

THE PEN OF MY AUNT

P. M. HUBBARD

SO FAR as I was concerned, the pen of my aunt was no joke, no sort of a joke at all. One stroke of it – or to be accurate the series of rather scratchy strokes my aunt put into her signature – could make all the difference to my life. Ah, but, you will say, the pen of your aunt was in this respect only a symbol, not an actual menace in itself. It symbolized, possibly, her power over you, but it was no more than a symbol. After all, you will say, she could write her signature, and so, if you are to be believed, make or mar your happiness, with any one of a dozen pens, or even, these days, with a ball-point or felt pen or some similar horror.

But that is where you will be wrong. You did not know my aunt, and you cannot know her pen, because no one who had not seen it could possibly imagine such a thing. The main part of it, the whole top four-fifths at least, was an actual feather, taken from an actual bird, and a big bird at that, but since dyed mauve. At least, I assume the dyeing, because I do not believe any bird, left to itself, has mauve feathers, certainly not a bird of that size. It would be altogether against the order of nature. The remaining one-fifth of its length was of gold or near gold, a slim barrel, which began by sheathing the quill and then turned into a sort of fountain-pen with a gold nib. It was not a real fountain-pen, because you could not pump ink into it, either by pressing a knob, as you do now, or by operating one of those small recessed levers the best pens had when I was young, or even by unscrewing either the nib or the quill and putting the ink in with one of those delicious little glass and rubber droppers, which survive now only for para-medical purposes. You could not put ink into it at all, or not on that sort of scale. It was what was called a long-writing pen, or something of the sort. It was a sort of half-way-house between an ordinary pen (if you can take your mind back that far) and a fountain-pen, and was used, I am sure, only by people who seldom went in for any very long writing. You dipped the nib in the ink for a moment, and it took up much more ink than a nib by itself could take up, because the nib had what was called a feed-bar under it, like a real fountain-pen, and the feed-bar stored up enough ink to enable you to write, perhaps, a dinner invitation or even a letter of condolence on the death of a not too near relative without dipping the nib back into the ink again.

Beyond that you needed an ink-pot. If one dip was going to be enough, you could simply unscrew the cap of your ink bottle and screw it up again after dipping. But if you were going to have to dip repeatedly, you really needed a proper open ink-pot, and there was one, once, to go with the pen. It was made of polished amethyst quartz with near-gold trimmings. There were other things too. They constituted what was called a desk-set, but I cannot remember what else the set included. I expect there was a paper knife. It was the sort of thing no one ever buys except to give to someone else, and you would not, even then, have given a present like that to anyone for whom practicality, let alone good taste, was a serious consideration. On the other hand, it was quite expensive, even then, and looked more expensive than it was. It was the sort of present you choose when the important thing is the fact of presentation, not the present itself. That was why, all those years ago, I gave it to my aunt. I gave her presents on her birthday and at Christmas. Never at any other time, because she did not need them – there was nothing, in fact, she did need – and because the giving was purely ritual and so required only on the ritually prescribed occasions. My aunt would have been displeased if I had not suitably observed these occasions, but otherwise did not want presents from me. The god Moloch would no doubt have been displeased with the Ammonite father who did not pass him his first-born through the fire, but would not in reason expect the thing to be carried any further down the family. And like the Ammonite father, I had confidence that, given the proper ritual presentation, the other party would play fair.

I do not know what happened, over the years, to the other components of my aunt's desk-set. She had servants, and she had no desk, and inevitably the other things, whatever they were, disappeared one by one. Whether or not my aunt observed their disappearance, I did not. But the pen remained, because it had the only nib my aunt could write with. She did not write much, but like all her generation she used writing as the normal means of communication with those outside the house. When she invited me to a meal, she sent me a postcard, and I replied on proper paper in a proper envelope. We were both on the telephone, but my aunt's telephone was for emergencies only, like a telegram. The pen, deserted by its original companions, lived in a drawer in the table in my aunt's sitting-room. A plain, small, screw-cap bottle of ink lived with it, rather like a paid companion living with a lady of rank who has outlived her own family. When my aunt wrote, she unscrewed the cap of the bottle, dipped the pen in the ink, screwed up the bottle again and put it back in the drawer. She must have known exactly how long the ink in the pen would last, and I am sure limited her correspondence accordingly. But it was not her correspondence I was mainly concerned with. It was her signature, on cheques and other prepared documents, and the amount of ink in her pen did not limit her performance there. She could have signed dozens of cheques and any number of codicils with one dip of the pen. But she did need the pen, or she could not, or at any rate would not, sign them. And after all, it was I who had given it to her in the first place. I had a right to question what she did with it, apart from my own interest in the matter, which was considerable.

My aunt's name was Mrs Brownlow. Only to me, of all mankind, was she Aunt Elsie. She had been a childless widow so long that you thought of her as a maiden lady, as if the Mrs was a sort of honorary title, such as used to be accorded to the housekeeper in the best houses. Only then I suppose her name would have been the same as mine, because she was my father's much older sister. I never knew what Mr Brownlow had been or what he had looked like. There were no faded photographs or moth-eaten pieces of military equipment, or if there were, my aunt did not have them on view. But if you sought Mr Brownlow's monument, you had only to look about you. Mr Brownlow had had a great deal of money, and now my aunt had it, and used it, very sensibly, for her own comfort and convenience. Even more sensibly, she used some of it, and could be expected to leave the rest of it, for mine. My father had neither made nor married much money, and when he and my mother perished simultaneously in a holiday shipwreck, I was left my aunt's only relative. I was already grown-up, but not earning enough to live on, and my aunt accepted responsibility for me. I have often thought that I had the sudden drama of my parents' disappearance to thank for this. If they had died later, of natural causes and one after the other, as might reasonably have been expected of them, I think she would have thought twice before taking me on, but in the excitement and confusion of the moment she did, and she was not a woman to let go once she had set her hand to the plough. Even so, there were no formalities, just what is called an understanding. Unlike most family understandings, this one was clearly understood, both by my aunt and by myself, and it worked very well until just after my aunt's eighty-seventh birthday, which was a fair run as these things go.

My aunt at eighty-seven was still formidable. She had been an Edwardian beauty, and there is no mistaking, at any age, the woman who has once known herself powerfully attractive. She was as tall and upright as a guardsman, but went in for floating, gauzy effects, as a mountain attracts clouds. She still liked mauve. She used to remind me of Shelley's waning moon:

Like a dying lady, lean and pale,
Who totters forth, wrapped in a gauzy veil,
Out of her chamber, led by the insane
And feeble wanderings of her crazy brain –

But I never said so, and in any case, it would not do, except for superficial appearances. My aunt was not insane in any possible legal sense, and her brain was not crazy or given to feeble wanderings. Her motivations, as she grew older, were increasingly unpredictable, but given her premisses her reasoning was impeccable, and she had a will of iron. It cannot be a coincidence that the age, *par excellence*, of the dominant and fun-loving man produced the most formidable array of women in the country's history. I only wonder if in their zeal for liberation the present-day women have not overlooked it. As to whether my aunt was dying, she was not, up to the time I have mentioned, or only in the sense that anyone of eighty-seven is obviously coming to it, and in that sense, in varying degrees, we all are.

Just after her birthday things began to go wrong, with her and with the understanding. Even then, there was nothing dramatic about it. My aunt did not have a stroke, or announce her forthcoming re-marriage, or suffer conversion at the hands of any of the more financially ambitious religious sects. Nor did I do anything to rupture our harmonious relations. There were no doubt things in my life which my aunt could not be expected to approve of, but none of these was suddenly revealed (if, indeed, my aunt did not know all about them already), and we had no sort of quarrel or open clash of interest. I had given her a present of the approved value for her birthday, and she had received it with apparent pleasure. Nevertheless, a week or so later she started looking at me.

This may not sound serious, but in fact it was, or at any rate disturbing. As you will have gathered, I saw her fairly often, and regularly (in the old-fashioned phrase which is so exactly appropriate) had my legs under her mahogany, but she seemed always to take my physical presence for granted. Not that there was anything in my appearance to attract her attention. On the contrary, I was always careful to be dressed, in her house, with the most inconspicuous correctness. But she never really looked at me in the way you generally look at the person you are talking to. She had large grey-blue eyes, which might once have been what were then called violet eyes, though I cannot believe that any woman ever had violet-coloured eyes, any more than I believe any bird had mauve feathers. She kept them very wide open (the fluttering eyelash did not come in until a good deal later and would not have been well regarded in my aunt's day), and moved them about a lot, as if she was perpetually and keenly aware of her surroundings, as indeed I think she was. But they never seemed to rest for long on anything near at hand, and she never used them as a means of communication. When she was talking to you, her eyes would be elsewhere, with an occasional quick glance at you, as if to make sure you were still there. Even when I was alone with her, she always looked at me as if I was a member of an otherwise unseen crowd, and it was the crowd rather than me that she addressed.

I think in some way I represented for her the entourage of male courtiers she had virtually grown up with. At least I was male, presentable, conversable and deferential to her wishes. The only other man she saw anything of was her solicitor, Mr Tarbert, and he did not fill the bill. No one could call him presentable, and if he had ever been male, it had been a long time ago. For the rest, the only conversation he ever had with her was to offer her advice, nearly all of which, I am glad to say, she rejected.

But about a week after her birthday this changed, and I found her looking at me almost as if she was seeing me for the first time and wondering what I came to be doing there. This was the more disconcerting in that it did not affect our verbal relations in any way. We talked as we had always talked (my aunt was a very considerable conversationalist), and much of the time she looked elsewhere as she always had, but when her eyes did come back to me, they really looked at me, even looked me over, with a critical and quite novel interest and at times this sort of surprise almost bordering on disbelief. I did not know what to make of it, and it made me very unhappy, the more so as I could not ask for any explanation. For that matter, I still do not know the explanation. I know now that my aunt had suddenly started to break up, and I assume that this was part of the process of dissolution. But what she was thinking when she looked at me like that I shall never know. Meanwhile, to look at and to listen to, she herself was as good as ever. That was where the danger lay.

I called again two days later, which was sooner than I should otherwise have done, but I was seriously worried. As I went up the steps, I met Mr Tarbert coming down. He has his brief-case in his hand, and I did not at all like the way he looked at me. With Mr Tarbert there was no surprise in this, because I never had liked the way he looked at me. The difference was that now he seemed almost pleased to see me, and I knew that if he was capable of deriving any pleasure from the sight of me, the pleasure could only be malicious. When I had passed him, it occurred to me to wonder whether the look on his face was one less of pleasure than of amusement, and that was the most disturbing thought of all. Nothing of the sort, of course, was said. On the contrary, we greeted each other politely, as we always did, and I enquired after my aunt, and he assured me that she was in the best of health. Nor was this necessarily disingenuous on his part, because when I met her a few moments later, I could see nothing wrong with her except the way she looked at me, which as usual she did not do very often. She did not remark on the earliness of my visit. I had an explanation ready in case she did, but she did not. Whether she noticed it I cannot say. We talked exactly as usual and after the usual time I left.

The next time I called, which was another two days later, the door was opened by Sally, not Paget. All my aunt's servants were women. Paget was the senior and most dislikable of them. She had been with my aunt since goodness knows when. She was her confidante and deputy, and would have been her evil genius if my aunt had ever permitted of such a thing. I think she was the only woman servant I have ever actually known still called by her surname alone. Sally was a new-comer and very different, so different that I did not know how long she would last. She was a plump, fresh-coloured girl, whom I found very congenial.

'I said, 'Hallo, Sally, where's Paget?'

'She's up with your aunt,' she said. 'Your aunt's poorly.'

'Oh dear,' I said, 'I'm sorry.' I was, indeed, sorry. I stood just inside the door wondering what to do.

Sally said, 'Shall I tell them you're here?' She said 'them' quite naturally, bracketing my aunt and Paget as if they were jointly her employers, which she may well have felt they were.

'Yes, please,' I said. I stayed there in the hall, partly because there was no point in my going any farther and partly because it gave me a pleasant view of Sally as she went upstairs.

When she came down, she said, 'Paget says she's ill and you can't see her.'

I felt sure Paget had not said this, but I felt equally sure that it conveyed exactly the effect of what she had said. I simply nodded. Then I said, 'Tell me, Sally, has Mr Tarbert been here?'

She looked very solemn at this. 'Not since the day before yesterday,' she said. 'He was here just before you.'

'I know,' I said, 'I met him. But he hasn't been since?'

'Not since,' she said, 'no.'

I left a suitable message for my aunt, though I doubted whether it would be delivered. I think I left it for Sally's benefit as much as anybody's. I knew I should be in again next day, but I did not say so. Sally showed me out, still looking solemn.

Next day it was Sally at the door again, and this time she seemed almost frightened, though I did not think she was a person who would frighten easily. 'Mr Tarbert's up with them,' she said. 'He's just gone up.'

Whatever it did to Sally, this certainly frightened me. I felt something of the helpless indignation of the man who has begun to suspect that the South African gold-mining scrip he has put all his savings in was printed in Buenos Aires. I did not know what I could do. I sent Sally up with the same message as the day before, and then, just as she disappeared round the bend of the stairs, I suddenly did know. I ran across the hall and into my aunt's sitting-room. I do not think I really expected to do anything more than perhaps gain a little time. I certainly did not contemplate for a moment the actual consequences of my action. When Sally came downstairs again, I was standing where she had left me, just inside the front door. She gave me the same reply as the day before, and I left.

From what Sally has since told me, I think it possible that my aunt died of rage, though of course the doctors did not say so. From what they did say, it is clear that she was dying anyhow. It was simply a matter of time. I had, as I have said, thought to gain a little time, but I could not know the full significance of the actual time I was gaining.

I saw Mr Tarbert at the funeral, but we did not speak.

The whole matter was very satisfactorily settled by correspondence. I, too, am very satisfactorily settled. Sally looks after all my needs, having been excellently trained in her duties, though not in all of them, by the now pensioned Paget. I miss my aunt, as a retired man is said to miss, in his new-found security and leisure, the stresses of his previous employment. But if you seek her monument, you have only to look about me. Nearly all that I have was hers. This must not be taken to include the pen with which I now write. All the same, it is a charming thing and I am much attached to it. It has a gold nib and a very dark purple plume. It has been dyed, of course. No bird could ever have produced a feather of such a deep, funereal purple, or certainly not one of that size. It would be altogether against the order of nature.

SCOTCH HENRY

GORDON McGILL

HENRY'S STOMACH was bothering him. It had been bubbling and squawling for a good half hour and it was putting him off his beer. Grrrrr, it said again, and Henry felt like Humphrey Bogart in *The African Queen* when ole Bogie was sitting down to tea with Katherine Hepburn and Robert Morley before there was all that shooting and before the leeches crawled up his legs. Bogie's legs, that is, not his, Henry told himself and smiled.

Another squiggle of bad air brought a belch to his lips.

'Pardon,' he said.

'Better out than in,' said Thomas.

'Aye,' said Richard.

For a week Henry had slept badly as he always did before the Annual General Meeting. When he was being honest with himself, he would admit that he hated the very idea of the trip south and this year was worse because he was taking vitamin C to fight a cold and the tablets didn't mix with the sleeping pills, giving him indigestion for which he took antacid which made him feel sick so that he had to buy port and brandies which he couldn't afford.

And the beer didn't help.

Thomas told him he didn't look well. The lack of sleep had puffed his eyes and the antacid had left a neat semi-circle of chalk over his top lip.

For a moment there was silence in the bar as Henry, Richard and Thomas gazed at their beers. Henry's glass slipped a fraction as he raised it and he rubbed the spilt liquid into his chin with the back of his hand.

'You're off then,' said Richard. 'Early, I suppose. To the AGM.'

Henry nodded.

'Will the Yank be there?'

'I expect so.'

'Queer buggers. Them Yanks,' said Thomas.

Henry smiled.

'You'll be in among the whores,' said Thomas. Hooo-ers, he said, blowing out the world like an owl.

Henry simply smiled again. Emily would have accused him of being patronizing, the way he just smiled.

Henry enjoyed a quiet drink at the bar. He felt at home. If ever a stranger came in, someone would make the introductions. But tomorrow night would be different. He'd have to slug back a couple of doubles before the words would come easy. And when he came back, he would be talking just a little bit like Herbie. He wouldn't say things like sidewalk or muthafucker or anything like that. But maybe he'd say address with the emphasis on the first syllable. And he'd ask for ice in his whisky.

Good old Herbie. Last year's best was: 'Here - I - am - in - a - singles - bar - y'know, - wearing - my - best - threads - because - I - keep - in - shape - so - I - can - still - wear - the - body - shirts. Anyway - I've - got - my - Bloomingdales - slacks - on - and - my - Eyetalian - boots – none - of - that - white - shoe - Miami - crap – so - I've - gone - to - a - lot - of - trouble - parting - the - hair - on - my - chest - and - hanging - a - goddam - tooth - on - a - chain - round - my - neck. Anyway, - I'm - there - and - this - Princess - is - there·

and - I'm - buying - booze - for - maybe - forty - minutes - when - her - girl-friend - comes - and - the - broad - says - scuse - me - my - lover's - arrived. MY LOVER, MY LOVER. You - think - this - feminism - is - all - political - you - know - from - nothing - cos - they - are - all - into - each - other - and - they - no - way - want - what - you - and - me - got - baby - with - the - penises - out - front. It's - all - ORALLY - STIMULATED - CLITORAL - ORGASMS . . .'

Another year, Herbie had said, and there wouldn't be a broad in Manhattan who wasn't a dyke and it was sure's hell going to spread to London.

Henry had practised all the way home.

'Load of crap,' Thomas had said.

'Right rubbish,' said Richard.

But Henry knew that they would both translate it to their wives who would sniff out a nonsense and then pass it on to the coffee-morning crowd and the Avon lady. In such a fashion, Henry held himself to be a chronicler of the world to the people of the town. It wasn't much but it gave him some standing. If not throughout the town, at least in the eyes of Thomas and Richard. Richard anyway, perhaps. And certainly it gave him some standing with Emily, which was all that mattered.

'Well, I'd better be getting away then,' he said.

'Get your head down,' said Thomas.

'Big day tomorrow,' said Richard.

Henry looked over his shoulder as he left and felt a small tickle of pride that he was the one to be going south.

And maybe this would be *the* year . . .

In Room 206 of the Strand Palace Hotel, Amy Rosenfeld flopped on to the bed and prised one shoe off a fat foot.

'I've been to see the Queen, Herbie,' she said to the bathroom door. 'Herbie. You in there, Herbie? Herbie, OI-BEE!'

The bathroom door opened and a face peered out, its nose dripping water. 'You don't shout in Europe, Amy. Didn't I tell you? Nobody shouts in Europe.'

'Go suck,' said Amy.

She took a breath, pushed herself off the bed and gazed at the mirror. Too fat, she said, and sat down again.

'The Queen wasn't in, Herbie. All this way to England and the Queen is out of the country. D'ya hear me, Herbie? There was no flag on the top of the palace. Meaning the old broad is out.'

Herbie reappeared, swathed in a robe and slapping lotion on his face. 'Did you have a good day, dear?' he asked.

'What we gonna do tomorrow?' she said in reply.

'I told you. We have lunch somewhere nice. I go to my meeting and at night we eat Italian in Soho with the guys.'

'Who guys? What guys?'

'The other delegates. Two English guys and a Belgian and Scotch Henry.'

'Do I get to fuck them?'

'They wouldn't have you.'

'Herbie,' said Amy. 'Sometimes I think that you think that I got a negative self-image. Whereas in reality, I have a warm generous go-out-and-get-'em personality.'

'You're talking clichés, Amy.'

'I love clichés. Nothing like a good cliché I always say.'

Herbie smiled and squeezed his wife to him. 'You are a stereotype. You know? A hunner-forty pounds of New York Jewish mixed-up ravenous man-eating cocksucker. And I love you.'

'So when do we eat?' said Amy.

It had been the best day of the summer. The young lovers were Clark Gable and Vivien Leigh that day. They had taken the bus eight miles into the country with their picnic hamper and they wandered out into a meadow beside a stream. A Donald Peers babbling brook. The sun stayed out all day. Bees, flowers, the scent of hay, the smell of the girl's hair. When he kissed her, she tasted of honey and when they made love she screamed once, twice, three times and almost crushed the boy in the strength of her passion. Henry had known nothing like it. Nothing could ever be like it. They were at one with the universe, spirits and bodies combined in a moment that could never happen again. They slept together naked in the meadow until the sun went down and then they dressed and walked back to the bus. There had never been a day like it and never would again.

Henry fastened himself into his seatbelt and yelped as he caught a pinch of belly fat between his thumb and the buckle. Quickly he cleared his throat and coughed. No one had heard him. He was sure of that. Reaching inside his jacket, he pushed his index finger into his breastbone and ran it slowly down his middle. Blip, blip, blip, blip. Four times. And blip again as he reached his crotch. I'm getting fatter and fatter, he thought. Should be jogging. Twice round the avenue in the morning and once at night. But I'd be laughed at. Besides, Emily doesn't mind. She would say it's immature to worry about a waistline after forty. Narcissistic. Possibly even latent homosexuality. Maturity meant coming to terms with physical decline. But maybe, thought Henry, I could get a rowing machine installed in the garage. Pretend to be rowing for

Oxford or crossing the Atlantic like Chay Blyth. In out, in out. Keep those knees together, soldier. Only three thousand miles to go. Pull them oars. Watch them sharks. Tote dat barge, lift dat bale, ya getta li'l drunk and ya lands in . . .

Henry coughed again.

Emily would have left by now. She wouldn't have bothered hanging on waiting for the plane to take off. She would say that it was silly to wave when she didn't know which window he was at or even if he was on the right side of the thing. She'd simply have gone home the moment she saw him climb the steps. Henry leant over the seat in front and peered through the window. Gone. Told you so.

Soon the girl with the black hair and the jeans would appear. The one reading *Playboy* in the departure lounge.

Henry practised his speech: 'I'm sorry but this seat is taken. It's been reserved by a fat old bore.' If she didn't react, he would say: 'He always sits next to me. He's fat and boring and talks to me all the way through the flight.' If she still didn't get it . . . but she would. A girl who looked like that would get it straight away. When she had settled herself, he would smile at her. Nothing pushy. Soon she would pick up the *Trident* magazine and flip through, probably stopping at the fiction. 'Why do all short stories begin on a plane or a railway compartment?' she would ask and Henry would tell her that travel is sexual. Strangers in a confined space. A brief acquaintanceship. A finite claustrophobic anonymous intimacy . . .

Henry dropped his eyes to his lap as the girl walked past and soon a farmer sat beside him and wished him good morning. As the plane took off, Henry gripped the seat and shut his eyes. Below him and ten feet to his rear, the undercarriage creaked upwards and locked with a shudder into the belly of the aircraft.

What if the wheels don't come down again, Henry muttered as he had muttered last year and the year before. Why can't they just let them hang there till we get to London?

As the stewardesses went through the safety procedure, Henry read his paper. Only first-time travellers actually watch the safety instructions. He glanced to his left. The farmer was watching.

Henry didn't enjoy his breakfast. Rubbery bacon. Not like Emily would have made. But he said 'Very nice thank you' when the stewardess took his tray from him and he smiled at the farmer. The flight lasted an hour and a half and, as they were landing, his palms began to sweat. He asked the farmer whether the undercarriage had come down.

'I don't know.'

'Did you hear it come down?'

'No.'

'Oh dear,' said Henry. He watched the farmer's face redden all the way down until the bump and the racing of the engines told them they were safe. For another year.

It took Henry only thirty minutes or so to feel at home in London. Each year the feeling of being a stranger decreased a little. There wasn't the same thrill as there had been eight years ago when he had danced on the escalators in Selfridges and said to Herbie, 'Look, Hamish, the stairs are moving.'

The conductor taking fares on the bus to the terminal was a West Indian. Henry smiled at him, and made a point of saying thank you very much. Foreigners prefer the Scots to the English. Everyone knew that. It's to do with humility and manners. Treating people as brothers.

Henry hoped the West Indian had caught his accent.

By the time the coach was swaying round the flyover by the Beechams sign, Henry felt at home. By the time he had had a shower in the hotel and stretched in his towel on the bed he reckoned he could have been a native. Still damp, he dialled home. The number rang and rang. Henry imagined Emily's eyes lighting up and her slippers scuffling across the floor with the dog leaping round her – a dervish-black creeper, twisting round her legs almost tripping her, trying to bite her nose. The phone rang and rang. She'd be wiping the earth from her hands or going back to the roses to make sure her spectacles weren't dangling on the bushes. Or maybe she had decided to lock the dog in the kitchen. Emily never worried how long the phone rang. If people wanted to talk to her, they would wait.

Ah, at last. How are you? Yes, I'm fine. Very nice flight. Nice breakfast. What? Cloudy, but no rain. Not for the moment. You got back all right from the airport? Yes, I know the traffic isn't bad but you're not the best at concentration, now are you?

Henry talked for ten minutes, asking what Emily would do that night. 'No, I'm not coming back on the sleeper tonight. We've had that out already. I'm booked on the morning flight. I'm not going to argue, Emily . . .'

As he spoke, he stretched on the bed, toes wiggling. He felt like Bogie in a motel scene, calling the Boys. Why couldn't he get an extension at home? A small luxury but it would be nice. Instead of standing out in the hallway staring out through the frosted glass into the avenue with every word being picked up in the living-room.

A kiss blown at the mouthpiece, and Henry dropped the receiver back on its cradle. Emily would go back to the garden. She'd let the dog out of the kitchen and it would leap and bark as if it had just been let out of Colditz. Henry fell asleep, and when he awoke he had to rush to make the AGM in time.

Everyone agreed that the dinner had been a success and it was Henry who decided they should go to a discotheque. Amy said okay. Herbie shrugged 'why not' and the two Englishmen muttered their apologies but they were going home. It was perfectly all right for strangers in town to go gallivanting, they said, but the natives had wives to go home to. The Belgian was drunk and had to be put in a cab back to the hotel. The firm had booked all the out-of-towners into the same hotel. So there was no problem.

The place Henry knew was five minutes' walk away and the three of them weaved through the Soho streets. Henry told his story. It was long and involved – all about his Dad who was a miner and hard-up all his life with never enough shoes to go round the kids' feet and one year he decided to go back to the Highlands where he came from and poach a salmon for Christmas. Herbie interrupted and said he would give his ass for culture like that, with all them bagpipes and oatcakes and that sonofabitch Rabbi Burns.

But Amy thought she had read the story before in a Book of the Month Club.

'So there was my father,' Henry was saying, 'fighting this forty-pounder in a stream and having to kill it with a rock. On his way home he slept with it under his head. 'Scuse me,' (bumping someone on the pavement) 'I didn't see ya, okay so I didn't see ya, so what's your problem pal? And on the road, it took him four days. Thieves kept cutting steaks from it so that he arrived with only about a third of the beast. But, man, we ate it just the same.'

'Man,' said Herbie.

Henry paid to get into the disco. He said he knew the manager but it seemed to cost him pounds and pounds to get the three of them inside.

Herbie and Amy danced while Henry drank and sang to the music. When they came back to the table Henry and Herbie talked about the AGM. It had been a waste of time. 'But I admired the lucidity of your report,' said Herbie. 'Everyone was most impressed by your lucidity.'

Henry nodded: 'In common with my countrymen, I possess the virtues of hard work, honesty, dedication and competency. Plus a sense of humour peculiar to my race and which doesn't travel.'

'I think you're funny,' said Amy.

'Peculiar but not ha-ha,' said Henry. 'Name me one comedian. One. Yours I could name hundreds. English I could name. Hundreds. Yiddish I could name. Name me one.'

'Harry Louder,' said Herbie.

Henry sighed and asked Amy to dance.

An hour later Herbie had fallen asleep at the table.

'I'm glad you came,' said Henry. 'Herbie didn't say he was going to bring his wife over.'

'Anniversary,' said Amy. 'A present for fifteen years of marriage.'

'Far out,' said Henry.

They left at three.

Henry and Amy helped Herbie into the taxi and guided him upstairs to room 206.

'Nightcap,' said Henry. 'Room 124.'

'Give me fifteen minutes,' said Amy and kissed him on the cheek.

Amy and Henry lay panting on top of Henry's bed.

'Well?' said Henry.

'There's no doubt that you are the worst lay in the world.'

'The earth didn't move?' asked Henry.

'Honey, the springs barely moved.'

'Oh well, never mind. Once it happened.' He told of the day in the field when the girl smelled of honey and there was a scream which tore through his soul. 'Ever since then her orgasms have been small sad silent things hissed into the sheets or coughed into the pillow, her head turned from me in shame.'

'That's beautiful. Small sad silent things.'

'I got it from a book.'

'Like the salmon story.'

'Yes.'

'I tried to describe it to Richard and Thomas once but I'd only just begun when they said it sounded like an advert for Corn Flakes.'

'They were right,' said Amy.

'Maybe I'll go to your room, wake Herbie up and tell him about us.'

'It wouldn't work, Henry. Haven't you heard? Jealousy is out. They've rationalized it away. Like religion.'

'Just one true moment of passion again. Before the fatness takes over. Just once. Transcending irony and absurdities. Just one more time. There must be one more time.'

'Herbie had it once when the Dodgers won the World Series.'

Henry sighed. 'Maybe I'll leap to my death off the GPO Tower.'

'You pass out before you hit the ground. It's a well-known fact.'

'I feel like the Savage in *Brave New World*.'

'Jesus,' said Amy.

'In the morning all this will sound silly.'

'It sounds fucking dumb now.'

Again Henry sighed.

'Well, I suppose you'd better be getting back to Herbie.'

Amy struggled out from under him, reached for her dress and groped for her shoes. As she zipped herself in, she turned back to the bed.

'Goodbye, Henry. Sleep well.' At the door she paused. 'There is no Emily, is there, Henry?'

From the bed came a soft voice singing: 'You must remember this. A kiss is still a kiss. A sigh is still a sigh.'

'Poor Henry,' she said as she closed the door and tiptoed gently out into the hall . . .

BREAD

PAUL MILLS

HE LOOKED at the clock again, between the girdered roof and the hot water pipes with their great iron knuckles, their twistings and turnings. In one hour his shift would be over. Through the gauze-covered open window he could see men on bicycles already going home in the rain-darkened evening. They passed in groups, many of them, larger than life on the shiny, wet road. From somewhere outside came the sound of cars roaring off from a standstill or swerving. Around him the faces in the lurid light looked tired, but everyone was in earnest to get the job finished. Pleased, he watched the last batch of bread on its way to the oven. A long canvas chute fed it piece by piece into hot tins as they rumbled past on a lower conveyor. He had spent too long that afternoon in the heat of the oven mouth, hauling out tinful after tinful, banging their contents on to canvas for the packers and throwing down empty tins with his gloved hands. His wrists were scarred from the hot metal. More than once the wide conveyor that passed through the oven had brought him too much to handle. The bread had stuck in the tins, outcoming tins had threatened to snag the machinery, he had panicked.

Even now he was still sweating. He sat at the opposite end of the sixty-foot oven, loading on lids as the tins passed. With or without lids, the tins lined up for a huge bar to pull them into the prover. It drew them in like small, black coffins with a clank of its arm, and a moving shelf hoisted them out of sight. Each shelf was long enough to hold a man stretched out. There was a smell of yeast and sweat. His arms ached and the working-time seemed endless. His thoughts seemed to jerk past him in a long line, repetitively. Though glad that the shift would soon be over, he felt ashamed and angry. The lids went on, but he failed to mind that they were loose. Then he had to run down to the other end to bring up more on an overloaded truck. No one spoke to him today as they usually did. No one joked about the girls outside, cycling past. It was the end of summer and everyone knew it. They were the regulars, and Christmas was their next spate of freedom, little at that. The nights drew in and time spread out, bringing nothing but clock-watching and foul language. One winter of dark dawns, one feverish summer, and the year was over. The men kept each other going just as much as the money. This had been one of his observations. Gripping a teacup and a cigarette, with the noise of the oven behind a wall, and the air relaxing round you even for ten minutes, was all you wanted. If there was a bit of conversation when you felt like it, so much the better. You could go home then, thinking that something had happened.

Among the men, his main friend was Spadeface. Management policy was for everyone to have a special job, even if that meant looking after the pig-house. Spadeface figured as a self-styled first-aid man. He was fifty years old, with a large, pale, square face, lined at the top with a bristle of grey hair. His most recent feat had been to extract and replace the amputated finger of one of the slicers, at whose fast-moving contraption Bill was now staring. As he looked, he could remember the amount of blood, and how the short, fat stump seemed hardly worth the fuss it had caused. But Spadeface had held it in his handkerchief as if it had been some rare, opulent butterfly. As time had passed, it grew obvious that the working morale of the bread plant depended upon Spadeface, even that of the two miserable Poles, though they were never certain, when he would ask them about their antics abroad, whether he was quite serious. Ugly as he was, he would often be found cuddling the women when they stopped with cups of tea.

At first, the bakery had appeared to Bill as a place where violent accidents were always imminent. Only gradually had he got used to the men's seemingly casual and unconscious avoidance of danger. There was the oven belt, dragging whatever it gripped into a tunnel of continual heat, the cat-walk above the merciless innards of the prover. Confectionery was stored in a huge fridge whose door could thud shut inaudibly, trapping the unwarned worker in a grey, frozen light. The pig-house too could be locked from the outside. There, at the end of the day, someone's job was to stack up large trays of dough and hacked-off loaves, musty tarts and leaking strawberries. Hundreds of mice lived there. They would sit up squeaking when you came in, or scutter, legs apart, over the floor. They and the mould gave a sweeping impression of greyness. Decayed cream dripped from rusty racks, and there was a thick, warm smell that seemed to have been there a long time. When the place was full to the ceiling, a pig farm would collect it: pigs would eat anything. The tumbrils where dough was mixed offered another fascination. These revolved at speed like open concrete mixers, while a fat, solid, metal fist jerked up and down inside. No weight or resistance could pacify it, as the dough was squeezed and pummelled, bursting and heaving. The fist, when stationary, reminded Bill of a picture he had seen of the face of a hammerhead shark.

Dangerous or not, the bakery demanded its price, and when Bill looked at Spadeface, he knew what that price was. Six days a week, ten hours a day, sometimes more, it absorbed you. Even Sunday had to be cut short to catch up on sleep until you were used to it. And when you were so entirely used to it as Spadeface was, you were old. From shift to shift the bread came through without stopping, twenty-four hours a day. Perhaps soon he too would become conditioned to this permanent and necessary situation. He would look towards it for excitement, interest, instead of looking beyond it, as now. He would stop hoping for some end or development. He would begin to think of the management as his parent-providers, good or bad, of the men and women as his brothers and sisters, even those he never spoke to. At that particular and sickening instant, it felt like being in hell, a hell whose only redemption was the occasional moment of warmth or friendship. The pay at the end was only a taste of that complete dependence he soon would be forced to accept all the time.

Two every second, the lids continued to clatter monotonously. Heat crawled over his skin like ants. Another truckload had to be negotiated at top speed, around steel supports and over wires, past men working. If he was too slow, tins would enter the prover without lids, and the bread would come out topped and voluminous, not boxed for slicing. Twice a day a huge batch of sliced loaves was required. The end of the shift would be marked by dough with currants. For these no lids were needed and he would go back to the oven end to stack tins for the day. Since it was Saturday, there would be no night shift. Work began on Monday at seven o'clock, when, after a week of heat, the oven had barely cooled. The slicers were taking the first of this batch from the cooler, a sign that the end was in sight. And, sure enough, currant dough began to drop off the belt into smaller tins. Bill's feelings eased a little as he strolled down to the oven. When he got there someone reminded him about the truck so he went back to fetch it. Each truckload took ten minutes to empty, and he had finished two since he last looked at the clock. He estimated that twenty-five minutes must have passed, so now he could afford another look. Twenty minutes only. He had been too generous. But now he could stack the tins, as a sign of conclusion, four crosswise then four lengthwise to a height of six feet or twelve tins. Full of bread the tins were heavy, weighing a stone each. But now they could be treated with contempt. Time had shifted a little in his favour. He greatly enjoyed his sense of speed and strength at the end of the day, lifting the tins automatically, as if his muscles were a machine that never wore out, but dealt with everything. His arms were brown from the summer sun, the heat of the factory, even from the golden dust that hung always in the air.

Spadeface stood at the oven, hauling out. His mate and one of the Poles were stacking hard. Each had an aluminium shovel to scoop staggering loaves off the conveyor, and slip them on to racks for cooling. If they did not work fast enough, bread piled on to the floor. This often happened as one of the men put down his shovel to manœuvre the laden rack out of the way and bring up another one. The whole factory worked on a conveyor system. Men filled the links machinery could not deal with. Outside, the rain had stopped. Rays of sunlight slanted through the gauze. A long, horizontal sunset tinted the dark clouds, across the far estates. Bill knew he should not let the outside world intrude too strongly into his mind when he was in the factory. But as soon as he breathed fresh air he was under its sway. The factory brought him to understand the bliss of relaxation and freedom, the sense of the outside and its strange innocence.

Yet even outside, recently, he had noticed a change. All time spent off work fled away so quickly that he hardly dared look at a clock. During his free time, he used to look at clocks with a sense of power. Yet his superior indifference had not lasted. When he was free, time ate away the hours. When he worked, it crawled. It was stubborn and had to be pushed along. This last forty minutes of the shift appeared to stand still, whereas outside they would have melted away. The men always talked about all that happened among families and friends outside work, as if that were really where they spent their lives. But as far as time went nothing could be further from the truth. Spadeface was talking about his fortnight in Blackpool, on the beach in the sun. To Bill this seemed nearly impossible to imagine, even the 'tarts on donkeys', which had somehow stuck in Spadeface's memory. His talk swaggered, his chest expanded, his gestures became agitated. He turned round and laughed while his hands worked on busily. One feeling united the men on the bread plant. It led at times to fury against those who did no work yet got paid for it. That was the idea that, like money, every second of their time off was earned.

Yet no man's loyalty belonged to the factory life, for all that. They each had a version of who everyone was outside, and this they believed in. Anyone who could not account for himself was suspect, and yet they never met nor took part in each other's lives outside. If Joe the Pole met Spadeface pushing his daughter's baby in the park, what would they say to each other? Bill could not imagine. Meeting at work seemed normal, even talking about the baby and the park, but meeting there incredible. Friendships all depended on the job of work, the mutual absorption in it, while what they actually valued lay outside it. They would go on strike, and had done so last spring. For three weeks the bakery had been idle. Money was useless in the factory itself, but vital for the time spent elsewhere. The leaders knew how to get the men to act. They appealed to their loyalty to each other, and they appealed to the justice of a good life off work. But somehow the two did not meet. Bill had looked at the monstrous, enamel oven, the conveyors, the tubs, the clock, and found that this loyalty was something the bread plant, the deadly contraptions, the whole system itself, had fabricated. To go outside and imagine the queues by bread shops, which were soon transformed into reality, did not make him feel easier in his mind, or that they were winning the battle. He had to queue up himself eventually. He had a distinct sense, while standing queueing, of every face wanting him back at work. Crushed lives had somehow become a necessity. Was the only hope therefore to oil the wheels and work as best you could? With this thought Bill continued to stack the trays. But the words grew muddled. Beyond a certain point he could not think.

'Hey Billy!' shouted Spadeface. 'Help me clean out them lights afterwards, all right?'

'Righto.'

He was not pleased, but could not refuse. It would mean overtime, half an hour perhaps. Had Spadeface asked him an hour or two ago, at the start of Bill's allowing himself to look at the clock, the thought of an extra half-hour would have been intolerable. Bill knew Spadeface had waited till the right moment.

Four neon strips lit the bread plant. Each was guarded by a minute, electrified fence, designed to eliminate flies from the working area. Insects attracted to the light would burn up on contact and drop in a long trough slung underneath. These periodically needed emptying. Overhead in the summer there was a constant sound of sparks, of burning and sizzling. Yet a fly in the bread would mean such bad publicity that no risks were taken. The apparatus worked because the insects never lost their urge to fly into the light.

Bill rested a moment and looked around him. The dough-men had already ceased cleaning the tumbrils, polishing them till not a stain was left. The flour-chute had been unhooked from the ceiling. It was almost six o'clock. The cleaners had herded debris to the middle of the floor. Someone walked past with a cartload of rejects, cakes and bread for the pigs. The stackers picked out buns hot from the oven with their bare hands. One of the Poles shook his hands and swore 'Bastards' as the currants burnt even his hardened skin. The man in a white coat swept by with a handful of papers. At his gesture the oven strangely altered its pitch of sound. Its rattling, energetic whine had become a drone, and the whole floor spread out in unusual silence. Bill felt hopeful at that moment, as if looking forward to something, he did not know what.

Yet suddenly a glimpse in front of him made him feel hopeless. The oldest member of the shift was stacking currant trays on to an unwieldy trolley. It tilted as their load and height increased. This man was even uglier than Spadeface. Years of effort had worn everything away but sinew and bone, yet he worked with the energy of an insect. His elbows and knees were merely knobbed spikes.

In the tight body the bones seemed rearranged wrongly. He was small and wiry, but worn out. Bill could not think of him sitting in an arm-chair, or wearing anything but his sweat-stained shirt, his turned-up, white trousers. The skin of his face was brown, drawn taut across the extremities, like a cooked chicken's. Bill noticed the exaggerated bone-structure, the nose, masculine and angular, where everything else had been sweated to nothing. Yet the man's eyes showed such bright, luminous intelligence. He was sixty-three. Bill wondered if whatever this man had hoped for had ever happened.

Already the scene was changing. With the last currant bun stacked for the vans, the men recognized the end of their shift. They began to drift towards the break-room to change. A couple of women were still washing cups near the big sink. Otherwise work had stopped. Bill's spirits were roused. He could postpone the pleasure of that triumphal walk that brought each week to a close. Tomorrow he would be free of the smell of bread and sweat. The laborious machinery also seemed to relax, clarified by emptiness. He sat on a pile of tins, his eyes closed. After a few oblivious seconds, Spadeface came back with a pair of step-ladders.

'Get me a bucket and sponge, Billy,' he said, 'and give it a dose of Domestos.'

He set the steps squarely under a light. One of the women brought him a cup of tea. Bill looked up, hearing the cup wobbling in the saucer. All other sounds but shouting were usually drowned. Gratefully Spadeface took it and slurped it down. The woman gave him one of her sourest looks.

'Dirty pig,' she said.

She grimaced and then smoothed herself.

'Hey, Mavis!' he called as she went away. 'Fetch one

here for young feller-me-lad.'

His voice echoed inside the empty plant like a foreign language.

'That was last cup. We're brewing another pot.'

She turned as she called, smiling right at them. Bill too went after her for the bucket. Mavis was a very quiet woman. Her face had a curious, wrinkled wash-leather look, yet it radiated a stern beam of kindness. She was small, thin and about fifty years old. She worked with another woman in confectionery. Whatever job they did they formed a twosome. Last year Mavis's husband had died, so the other women showed her a kind of respect. She and her friend often whispered in confidence together, and though they were always sociable, no one could quite intrude. Bill searched for the bucket under the sink. He had worked in confectionery himself at first. The bread plant had been a rise in masculine status. Some of the girls also stayed behind to wash up. Big bowls soaked on the long drainers. Ladled handles sprouted out of the water. Bill liked talking to the older women. They seemed to have matured into a strange hen-like placidity. The younger ones were cooler but more interesting. They swopped friendships spitefully, but with the boys they either attempted bitchiness or let it be known that they were accessible. By far the prettiest was a girl with an artificial leg. Her leg had been amputated in a car accident.

Bill chatted to the girls as they left, already breathing an air of Saturday night. His hands tingled, scorched by drops of Domestos, as he carried the bucket back to Spadeface. He set it down by the steps, watching the water balance. On the top step Spadeface unhooked the trough. His eyes were wet from the glare as he looked down. Bill quickly ran to turn off the light.

'You're a bright spark. You should be in that office.'

Even though Spadeface regarded Bill as a sort of clean slate on which he could imprint his opinions, this was not the first time he had made this remark, and it was a point about which they disagreed. He had never managed to say why, but becoming one of the bosses appealed to Bill very little. Because he enjoyed his leisure so much, he regarded the management, since they had more, as men who got fat on others' sweat. He looked at the silent factory now as a tortured man released from the instrument of his punishment, who could survey the levers and wheels in peace, knowing he had survived. He had learned not to live in the future.

Together they cleaned the trough, rinsing the cloths. Spadeface as usual did most of the talking. This time, however, he surpassed himself. He began telling Bill about his daughter, about the time she was born. He began to describe the birth; what had happened. As he talked it dawned on Bill that Spadeface kept this memory well locked up. Many children had been born at home in those days, though few actually delivered by the father. Perhaps this had been the one, absolute moment of fear that Spadeface had ever known. It had happened too quickly for any practical, let alone mental, preparation. With hands that pulled bread out of the oven every day of the week, Spadeface had lifted the baby into life. As he talked, Bill pictured it vividly, and this in itself proved an altogether strange experience. Yet in another way it seemed totally normal, only strange because of their surroundings. There had been so much blood, real scarlet blood. Then a feeling of ecstatic relief and delight. The delight, Spadeface said, had lingered on for days, like shock. He spoke of it in a tone almost of confession.

Dusk had fallen, with its scent of leaf-mould and grass.

Spadeface stood at the window, breathing it. Then he got back to the cleaning operations.

'Time for the night shift, any other night,' he said.

They hoisted another trough down. It was full of flies. It took them ten minutes to get off the grime. Billy went over to get some clean water, while Spadeface climbed back up with the trough. He was having difficulty hooking the chains in place when Bill arrived. The last hook had twisted. Just as he got it back, the steps wobbled. Bill suddenly thought Spadeface might fall. He heard the creak of the rope that joined the angles of the steps together. He thought of Spadeface impaled on the conveyor, and himself running for help.

'Mind it,' he said.

Bill's foot steadied the steps as Spadeface came down. They moved over to the last trough. After the wires were cleaned, this one unhooked without any trouble. Bill switched on the other lights, so that Spadeface could see what he was doing. A big moth, extracted from the wires, dropped to the floor. Spadeface scraped odd flies into the trough, then brought it down. He balanced it evenly, stepping carefully. Bill footed the ladder. When they had finished, the four troughs sparkled with a gleaming enamel whiteness. Then they clocked off, not speaking, in an easy silence.

THE INTERVIEW

GRAHAM PETRIE

'YOU CAN go in now,' the secretary told them, and the three men glanced at each other uneasily before rising, each of them waiting for another to make the first move. Finally the eldest of them took the initiative, a burly man of about fifty who had refused to take off his coat and had sat with it unbuttoned, his hands planted stolidly on his knees, the coat tails drooping to brush the floor. He rose slowly to his feet and led the way towards the door.

Inside the office they found themselves facing a large desk made of some dark plastic substance treated to resemble wood; behind the desk sat a man and a woman. Neither paid much attention to the newcomers: the man, who was balding and nearing fifty, held the end of a pencil between his teeth and tapped them thoughtfully as he gazed towards the window; the woman, a blonde of about thirty, wearing jewelled spectacles that swept upwards at the rims, stared at them briefly and with some hostility before directing her gaze to the pile of papers that lay on the desk before her. The three men hesitantly approached the row of hardbacked chairs that faced the desk and paused, waiting for an invitation to be seated; when neither person behind the desk paid any further attention to them, they followed the lead of the man with the coat once more and sat down.

There was another pause: the woman shuffled briskly through the papers as though searching for something, while her companion remained fascinated by the view of the sky through the window, and the regular click of the pencil against his teeth began to create a subtly disquieting effect. The two younger men looked to their leader for guidance, and he seemed on the point of registering some preliminary remark when the man behind the desk suddenly became aware of their presence.

'Well?' he demanded.

His voice conveyed boredom, irritation, resentment at the intrusion on his privacy that they represented. The man who had been about to speak looked startled: he straightened up in his chair and placed his hands on his knees once more.

'Well,' he replied, 'we're all here to be interviewed for the same job, aren't we? I would have thought – ' he hesitated, looking round at his companions – 'that you would have taken us one at a time, instead of all together – '

'It's not your business,' the man interrupted, 'to worry about *our* motives. *We're* here to look into *yours*. Do you understand?'

'Yes, I see,' the spokesman muttered, totally discomfited. He glanced at the woman for assistance, but she responded with a glance of such overt, frozen dislike, that he decided to retreat utterly from the role that had been forced upon him and huddled back into his chair, drawing the edges of his coat together to shield him.

The interrogators exchanged a contemptuous smile at this easy triumph and transferred their attention to the man sitting on his right, who was about ten years younger and boasted a drooping, robber-baron moustache and thick sideburns.

'And what have you got to say for yourself?' Once again there was naked hostility behind the question.

'Me? I'm looking for a job that requires creativity, original thought, energy. My name's Manfred Garmes. I worked for IBM for six years, but I got tired of the routine, the impersonality. I want a fresh start – '

'We're not interested in the inadequacies you perceived, or claim you perceived, in your previous jobs. We want to know about your capacity for *this* one.'

'All right,' Garmes replied, taken aback but willing to accommodate himself to the requirements of his future employers. 'I've got some very clear ideas about deployment of resources in an organization like your own. I think it's possible to eliminate waste and unnecessary expense by introducing changes in selected areas that would cause a mimimum of disruption to the overall pattern. I've thought this over very carefully and – '

This time it was the woman who interrupted. 'Another new broom,' she laughed contemptuously. Her voice was cold and brittle and she did not even deign to look at Garmes as she spoke. 'Haven't we had enough of these? People with no idea of the practical problems involved and yet are going to make everything perfect overnight?'

Garmes was about to defend himself, for, after all, this was a distortion of the deliberately guarded remarks that he had originally made, when the third of the candidates for the job spoke up for the first time. He seemed the least impressive of the three, a small, already stooping young man of about thirty, with pale watery eyes peering from behind rimless glasses; and yet his voice held unexpected authority and passion.

'Don't bother about them,' he said to Garmes, 'they'll twist everything you say and throw it back at you until they've got you utterly confused. That's what they're here for, that's their job. They call it psychological testing, I've heard about it before. First of all they get at each of us in turn and try to make us feel inadequate and helpless. Then they set us against each other, for only one of us can get the job and we're all supposed to probe each other's weaknesses and humiliate each other. And then finally they make some mysterious, arbitrary decision that one of us has shown more 'character' or 'competitiveness' or 'resilience' than the others and he gets the job. I think it's disgusting, and I vote we don't let them get away with it. Let's just ignore them and talk among ourselves until they decide to treat us like human beings.'

He glanced at his companions for approval and received a quick nod from the man in the coat, who had come back to life as this denunciation gathered force and had now regained something of the alert and decisive air he had shown at the beginning of the session. Garmes seemed more reluctant: he had come prepared for a battle of wits of the kind that had just been developing and he regretted giving up the chance to shine at the expense of the others, both of whom he had already decided offered him little challenge. He accepted the proposal nevertheless, confident that he could still turn the new situation to his own advantage.

'That's fine,' the young man said. 'If they want to speak to us, all they have to do is to ask politely. Meanwhile let's find out something about each other.

'My name's Duggan, Elwood Duggan. I don't like it, never have done, but it was my mother's maiden name and she insisted on giving it to me. Maybe I'd have got on better with her if I'd been called Joe or Fred, but it's too late to think about that now. She passed away a year ago.'

Garmes muttered some conventional noises of sympathy

and Duggan paused to acknowledge them. 'Thank you,' he said. 'It's very kind of you, even if you never knew her. She was a good woman in her own way, but very domineering. I resented that, of course, especially when I was a young man and she would object to any girl I tried to bring home and introduce to her. I always blamed her for the failures I had with women, though I can see now that they were my own fault too, probably mostly my fault. It was up to me to break away from her once I realized what was happening. In any case all that's far in the past now, and what matters is the present. I miss her more than I thought I would, though, now that she's gone.'

He paused, as though realizing that he was in danger of embarrassing his listeners. 'But I'm doing all the talking,' he said, 'and really I'm a very dull person, nothing worthwhile has ever happened to me. What about you,' he went on, turning to the man in the coat, 'Mr . . ., I'm afraid I don't know your name yet? I expect you're a married man, not like myself?'

'Carter,' the man replied, 'Donald Carter. Yes, I'm married. Two children, one seventeen, a girl, just got engaged two weeks ago. The other's a boy, fifteen, still at high school. I say to my wife, Brenda's far too young to be married, and then she reminds me she was only nineteen herself and we've done well enough. It makes you think though.'

'And you?' Duggan prompted, looking at Garmes.

'Married or not married, what does it matter?' Garmes replied, aware that the woman behind the desk had secretly been noting down the previous conversation. 'Why do people always feel they have to start off by exchanging banalities about wives and mothers and children? No offence meant, but can't we talk about something more significant, before you all start digging out your family photos and showing them around?'

'What do you consider significant then?' asked Duggan mildly.

'Well, we came here to look for a job, didn't we? We must have some ideas about work, mustn't we, and the place it has in our lives? You for example,' turning to Carter, 'you have teenage children, old enough to start looking for work if they want to. Do they? Do they want to work, or have they abandoned the work ethic already? Most of the young people I know don't want to work and, in a way, I sympathize with them. They're more open than we are, more spontaneous, they're concerned about other things than the size of the weekly pay packet and buying a second car and a colour TV. Not that this attitude doesn't have its dangers, I can see that, and yet it's somehow refreshing too. Meanwhile those of us who are just that little bit too old to take part in that freedom – and yet in a very real way we helped to make it possible for them – we have to go on working. Fortunately in my case it makes very little difference, I've always thrown myself heart and soul into any job I've taken, and I've always obtained a great deal of satisfaction from my work. But I'm sure other people haven't been so lucky.'

He paused and waited for Carter to respond. 'Well,' the older man began slowly, 'in some ways it's like the way you put it, sure enough. I've argued it out with them, Brenda and Davy, but they tell me I'm just an old fogey who doesn't see it like it is – that's the way they put it. I've always had to work, all my life, ever since I was fourteen, so I find it difficult to see things the way they do. They've always had it so easy, never had to struggle like we had. I don't grudge them it, that's what I always wanted for them after all, yet I often think a bit more discipline wouldn't have done them any harm. That's the trouble perhaps, they've no authority, no one they can look up to, respect.'

Garmes was unable totally to conceal a smile of contempt at this: 'That's the easy answer, isn't it?' he said. 'More authority. Tell them what to think. Don't ever give them the chance to work things out for themselves, in case they come up with answers that show you how useless your own life has been. And then blame it all on society, to cover up your own inadequacies as a parent. It's not society's fault if there's no one to look up to, no one to respect – it's yours.'

Carter was about to protest that this was not what he had been trying to say at all, when Duggan gently recommended that they change the subject. 'This is exactly what they want us to do,' he reminded them, nodding in the direction of the two psychologists, who had quickly reassumed their elaborate façade of boredom and indifference. 'Even if we *are* competing for the job, there's no need to degrade ourselves by falling into the trap they've set for us. That's the enemy over there, not Carter or Garmes or myself. Let's remember that.'

There was a moment's silence while the two other men tried to think of a more neutral subject to discuss. Garmes, however, was secretly elated: he felt that he had begun to impose an image of himself as forward-thinking, open-minded, and yet responsible, aware of the dangers of proceeding too fast and without paying adequate attention to all the possible consequences. He waited patiently for the more sluggish mind of Carter to come up with a new topic of conversation, but it was Duggan who finally got things going once more.

'I've been reading a very beautiful book lately,' he told them. '*Siddartha*, by Hermann Hesse. Do either of you know it?' Garmes nodded, and Carter shook his head. 'It made me realize how little value we generally place on the spiritual things in life,' Duggan continued musingly. 'How little it is we *really* need to be contented. It was recommended to me, strangely enough, by a young lady I met in a bar. Don't get me wrong, it was a very respectable singles bar, not like some other places I could mention. I was sitting drinking my orange juice – that's all they serve there – and she came up and asked if she could join me. I was a bit suspicious at first, but she told me that she was just looking for someone to talk to, and she thought that I looked the right type. She said she had been there for half an hour already and all the men she had met had done nothing but ask for her telephone number or suggest that they should drive her home.

'Anyway we started to talk and found we had a great deal in common. We were both lonely and we both wanted more than a cheap, casual relationship. That was when she told me about *Siddartha* and suggested that I read it. I bought a copy the next day.'

'And when you were finished talking, I suppose you offered to drive her home?' sneered Garmes, eager to establish the worldly-wise persona that he felt was essential to success in the business community.

'Oh, no,' responded Duggan, startled. 'Nothing like that at all, I assure you. Certainly I wanted to see her again, but I wasn't going to be like the other men she had told me about and ask for her telephone number. That would have been degrading, both to her and to me, after what we had shared together.'

'So what did you do?' asked Carter, who had belatedly begun to take an interest in the story.

'I did it the other way around. I gave her *my* telephone number and told her to call me if she wanted to see me again.' Garmes gave a snort of amusement, but Duggan went on earnestly: 'I've always felt it was unfair that it should be the responsibility of men to initiate and follow through a relationship while the woman has to remain passive and not take any steps on her own.' He smiled deprecatingly. 'I suppose I felt I was doing something on behalf of Women's Liberation.'

'Oh, brother!' Garmes sighed, apparently to himself, yet loud enough for the couple behind the desk to overhear. 'Has it never occurred to you,' he continued, addressing himself to Duggan, 'that women have their own way of letting men know that they're interested in them? It's got nothing to do with social conventions at all. If they want you, they let you know all about it, don't worry about that.' He laughed complacently. 'I can vouch for that from experience.'

'And *did* she call you?' Carter enquired sympathetically.

'Not yet,' Duggan admitted. 'But it's only been a week since I met her. She's probably been busy. She said she was a teacher. But I'm certain she *will* call me.'

'Probably has to wait till her husband's out of town again,' suggested Garmes.

Duggan was shocked. 'Oh, no, I'm quite sure she wasn't married. She would have told me if she was. She wasn't that kind of person at all.'

Garmes laughed once more: 'You sure don't know much about women,' he informed him, 'if you think she would tell you that kind of thing. Not that I,' he added, glancing cautiously at the desk, 'would ever get myself mixed up with someone who was married. I've got too strong a sense of self-preservation for that.'

Duggan noticed that Carter had begun to look uncomfortable, as though there was something he wanted to say, and yet he hesitated to come out with it. 'Is there anything the matter?' he enquired sympathetically.

'No . . . no . . . nothing,' Carter muttered, obviously preoccupied. Duggan waited, smiling at him encouragingly, and this seemed to assist the older man to speak.

'It's nothing that would interest anyone else,' he began cautiously. 'Purely a personal matter. Only when you were talking about married women picking up men in bars . . .' He paused, once more avoiding Duggan's eye, while Garmes shuffled his feet impatiently and threw back his head to stare up at the ceiling. 'Well,' Carter went on, with a sudden rush of confidence, 'you've been honest with me and I need to talk about it with someone. Sometimes you can tell things to strangers you can't talk about with anyone else. I haven't even told my kids yet. I don't know *how* to tell them.'

He glanced at Duggan again, almost appealingly, and the younger man made a gesture with his hand as though to place it on Carter's arm, then thought better of it and smiled once more instead.

'It's about my wife, you see,' Carter continued, reassured. 'They think she's gone off on vacation for a few weeks, but really she's left me. We've been married for twenty-three years, last Sunday, and now she's gone off with another man.

'And that's not the worst of it. She told me things before she left, hurtful things. I don't know whether to believe them or not, maybe she just meant to hurt me with them. She said this wasn't the first time either. There had been other men, lots of them, even just after we were married.'

He paused and glanced anxiously at his companions, fearful of how they would respond to his humiliation. Garmes avoided his eyes; he was whistling very softly and tapping his teeth with his thumbnail, in a possibly unconscious tribute to the indifference of the man behind the desk. Duggan, however, smiled and nodded his head for Carter to continue and the older man went on with a rush, the words becoming blurred and confused as he neared the end of his story.

'She said I had never satisfied her, not really satisfied her, even when I was younger, and so she had to go to other men. Brenda and Davy, the two kids, she said they weren't mine at all, I wasn't capable of making them she told me, and she had to find a real man to do it for me.

'She said she couldn't even remember now who the fathers were, it could have been any one of half a dozen men. And she'd stayed with me all this time only because I was too blind to see what was going on and I earned enough to make her comfortable. Well, she'd had enough of it now, and I could look after the kids; seeing that I'd always been so proud of them, I might as well have them.

'It was just last week she told me this, as soon as I told her that the company had redundancies and it was some of the older men who had to go. She was still young enough, she said, she had a life of her own before her and she wasn't going to throw away the chance to make the most of it. What do you think of that for an anniversary present?'

The man tried to smile at them as he finished speaking, but in reality he was almost weeping and had to lower his eyes quickly to hide the tears that were forming in them. He shook his great head heavily from side to side, but kept his hands placed firmly on his knees, gripping them tightly. Duggan made the gesture with his hand once more and this time reached Carter's arm and patted it consolingly. 'Try not to worry about it,' he told him uneasily. 'Maybe it isn't true, maybe she was just trying to hurt you for some reason. People often say things like that and then regret it later. You'll see, it'll still work out for you, I'm sure it will.'

Carter merely shook his head helplessly, while Garmes continued to stare at the ceiling and to whistle softly through his teeth. But the woman behind the desk had been rapidly noting down the details of Carter's confession, and now the man whispered something in her ear as she wrote.

Duggan became belatedly aware of the couple's activities and hastily got to his feet, his face flushed with embarrassment and anger. 'What have you been doing?' he demanded heatedly. 'You've no right to record that kind of thing, no right at all. It's a breach of confidence. This was a private conversation. I insist that you tear up these notes at once. If I'd known this kind of thing would happen, I would have warned the others to leave immediately.'

The man behind the desk stared at him blandly and said nothing, while the woman, after a brief glance at the intruder, resumed her note-taking. Duggan took a step towards the desk and stood there, fists clenched, his arms dangling by his side. 'I insist that you hand over these notes,' he repeated helplessly. The man continued to stare at him indifferently and abruptly Duggan turned away, his body almost visibly crumpling as he did so and taking on once more the stooped, frail appearance that, for a brief moment, it had overcome.

'Let's go,' he muttered, taking Carter's arm and leading him towards the door. Garmes remained seated till they had almost left the room, then he rose slowly to his feet, shrugged his shoulders, and began to follow them. He paused, however, as he came level with the couple behind the desk. 'You can see that none of this is my fault,' he explained in a conciliating tone, 'I had nothing to do with it. I'd be willing to return for another interview any time that suits you.' The man nodded at him curtly, but his lips were compressed in an expression of distaste that did not augur well for the future.

It was raining as the three men came out of the main entrance to the building. Garmes ignored his companions and did not even offer a farewell: he set off rapidly to claim his car from the company's parking lot. Carter said that he would take a bus. Duggan began to accompany him, but after a few paces he remembered that he had left his briefcase in the office and that he would have to return to collect it. Carter shook him warmly by the hand and thanked him for his assistance, but the younger man could only apologize for the disaster he blamed himself for causing. He ran back to the building and took the elevator to the fifteenth floor. He walked briskly through the outer office, nodding to the secretary as he passed, and found the couple still sitting at the desk, comparing notes. The man rose to his feet as he entered and stretched out his hand towards him: 'Fine work, Dr Duggan,' he congratulated him humbly. 'There's no doubt at all now which one's right for the job.'

NINETEEN POLICEMEN SEARCHING THE SOLENT SHORE

GILES GORDON

SAW THEM, nineteen of them, their eyes to the ground, walking towards the sea. But the sea was not approaching them. It, presumably, had other fish to fry, or something of the sort.

Canute-like, the waves retreated before us, said the first policeman, his back view, the microphone placed somewhere strategic, the tape-recorder somewhere within the microphone. Never mind that it was the waves which retreated, not Canute.

And the second muttered: until the water surged back, saturating our turn-ups. Salt water, of course it was, and the salt is still on my trousers. The old woman pointed that out to me.

Evidence of a sort, said the first.

It would be, were we being examined, said the second.

These days, who knows when we will be, said the third, and there was a little wry laughter. It began to echo, the laughter, then was lost against a hollow sound, as if water were slapping into a cave, waves and more waves taunting the shingle, then rasping back from it.

Nineteen policemen walking towards the sea. For why? Why? Not all of them in uniform, maybe – ah, this hadn't occurred to me before now – none of them in uniform. A closer inspection revealed gum boots, trousers tucked into same, warm, woolly, winter sweaters. But not these habiliments on all, you understand, otherwise no turn-ups would have been soaked.

The fourth policeman said (assuming they uttered in the order in which they lined up to face the sea, the oncoming or retreating tide, which was not repeat not the case): policemen do not have turn-ups on their trousers.

Discuss, said the second.

Touché, said the fifth, who was wearing (his body in shadow, vaguely a dark, male form) nondescript garments, chosen for a working day by the sea. But so were they all, most of them. Practical clothes.

They walked towards the sea. The tide was out. They could hear the water, hear the sea sounds, the gulls, the other sea birds, feel the squelch of wet foreshore, hear the rattle of water running away from pebbles, smell the seaweed, the tang of wet salt, the sea smells, with their eyes shut, even with their eyes shut.

Though none of us had our eyes shut, said the sixth. What would have been the point of that? If you have eyes, you might as well make full use of them.

The sixth was a little farther away from the first five than they were to each other. In the picture, the photograph, I've ringed him there, there, look, a little ahead of the others, a few millimetres nearer to the water's edge than the rest, nearer the objective.

Or farther from it, said the eighth, a bitter man, no longer competitive, perhaps because once he had been more competitive, more ambitious than any of the others, were it possible to make such a comparison between these nineteen policemen (any nineteen policemen), which it is not.

The seventh? At this point he was silent. Which neither meant that he was more intelligent or observant than the others, nor less so, could such measurement be employed, were it considered (by a *deus ex machina*) worth applying it.

No, I wouldn't mention his name. Nor my own. Nor the names of any of the others. Assuming I knew them. Some of which I did, but not all. Said the ninth. Of course we all had names, have names. We're people, aren't we? Human beings, with all that that implies. Not just men in blue (not that we were wearing blue, most of us, or if so only incidentally), not just back views, not just nineteen –

Who's been counting us? What's the point of that? said the tenth.

But, went on the ninth, in this context, in the context of now and the photograph, of then and the photograph, we are just nineteen back views in search of, in search of . . .

And he couldn't or wouldn't complete the sentence, a sentence that was of his own beginning and of his own making. Disgusted? God, yes. Speechless? Had become so. Hadn't he?

Hadn't we all, said the eleventh.

They went on walking towards the sea. The wind and cold bit. The sea was still retreating. How many paces had they taken? Maybe they were not moving as quickly as they gave the impression of doing.

Mass baptism. Complete immersion. Communal conversion. Is that what you think we're about? said the twelfth. You don't believe that? You couldn't.

A slightly ribald ripple of laughter along the line,

beginning about the middle, the ninth or tenth man, and spreading towards each end but ending before it arrived there, dying out, fading away two or three men from each end, where precisely extremely hard to pinpoint. Were it important it could probably be done.

Probably? said the thirteenth. A lot of things are probably. Fewer than possibly, though. That you must grant. That's how it goes. The difference in force and impact between the words. Emphasis is all.

Their eyes were on the ground, on the mud, the shingle, the shore. Their bodies cast thin shadows almost directly behind them, which indicated the time of day, though at different times during their search their shadows would have been at quite different angles. The sucking and mewing and glugging and globbing of the wet on dry, the salt water turning the sand – was it sand or merely dirty, smelly mud or silt? – into an inchoate, shiny surface, a momentary smooth texture to be broken by large feet, bigger boots and shoes.

That, said the fourteenth, doesn't need saying. Shouldn't be said. Stands to reason, the shoes and boots housing the feet must –

Per se, said the fifteenth, an aspirant to more private matters –

Be larger than the feet which they contain, continued the fourteenth, ignoring the almost silent interjection. Houses are bigger than the people who live in them, he added unnecessarily.

But God is bigger than a cathedral, said the fifteenth, not a logician.

22 July 1974. The date was, is, unimportant; or, and no paradox is intended, important. Either way, in this context it is irrelevant, but 22 July 1974 was and is the date. Perhaps it should be documented for those who

appreciate this kind of documentation. It could, you understand, have been any date, even a Saturday or a Sunday, but it was that date. 22 July.

The sixteenth. Policeman. You remember that they are policemen, that they're all policemen, though back views are what we're concerned with? Yes? Of course you remember. Anything *you* say may be taken down and used in evidence against . . . Of course, you know all that. And, these days, you never know. These days? And what does that imply?

The sixteenth thought, perhaps spoke. Some of these words thought, some spoken. Walking towards the sea. Don't like to get my feet wet. At any time. On duty or off. With my mates or with the wife and kids. Even when making sand-castles, try to keep the feet dry. I don't mind particularly, and if I'm wearing wellingtons, as I was that day, the chances are, if the rubber behaves itself, all will be well. But for choice I don't like to get them wet. Not my idea of a holiday. But not a holiday, I agree. Work. On the job. A change from flashing my gloved hand at traffic or beaming a torch into dingy corners. Not that I've done that for a while. On the beat? This? Some beat. Immersed in water. Would I float? Hold my nose, press nostrils together, clasp fingers on either side of the flesh, no air getting in. Mind you, none escaping either. Dial 999. The call would misroute from under the water. Drowned in the course of executing his duty. A requiem mass, if he believed in Mozart.

July 22nd 1974. Nineteen policemen – maybe more but nineteen are nineteen, a reasonable body of men, each witness to the presence of eighteen others – walking towards the sea, towards the ocean, the water, the slopping great bowl, basin of liquid, the depths, for reasons best known to others.

Was the day grey? It looked it from the photograph I saw but this may have been photographic licence, or dirty work in the darkroom.

We were looking down, not up at the sky, said the seventeenth. Had we been looking up, at the ostensible blue, it is improbable that our mission would have succeeded, to phrase it politely.

And did it?

Refuse to comment, refuse to comment, refuse to comment, refuse to comment.

Comment is sacred. Facts are ten a new penny.

New pennies are no longer new. Tarnished and devalued.

Refuse to comment, refuse to comment, refuse to comment, refuse to comment.

I'd put to you the following, said the seventeenth: had the day been bright and hot, summery in the true sense and not just that it was on paper a summer month, would we have been garbed as we were?

The clothes you were wearing could have had more to do with the nature of the job in hand than with the temperature and conditions.

That's reasonable, responded the seventeenth, though there must be a happy medium. Somewhere.

Did he know what he meant by that, or was it a cliché from the book, from some manual of instruction? The weather forecast in *The* (London) *Times* the previous day for that area of England had read (in part): mainly dry, rather cloudy; wind SW, moderate or fresh; max temp 21 degrees C (70 degrees F).

Said the eighteenth, commenting upon the day's activities: The weather was mainly dry, rather cloudy. The wind was south-westerly, moderate or fresh I'd say. The maximum temperature was 21 degrees centigrade, which is 70 degrees fahrenheit.

The question inevitably arises: was he wasted in the force, had he missed his vocation as a weather prophet? The answer, equally inevitably, is no, he was far from wasted. The police force requires its specialists, its experts, as already indicated. Without them, it is but . . . what it is.

Asked the nineteenth, the last man, hands clasped behind his back, he and the man next to him, the eighteenth, both wearing white polo-necked sweaters, all the others in dark clothes: Did you and your colleagues speak to each other?

Someone said: colleagues? I hadn't seen most of them before, and I couldn't recall having previously spoken to any of them.

The eighteenth searched the shore with his eyes, as did the others. All those faces facing downward. Maybe his concentration on the task in hand was such that he hadn't heard the question, or been able to absorb it. Maybe he preferred not to answer.

The question was repeated: Did you and your colleagues talk to each other, while on the beach?

They walked . . . relentlessly, so it seemed. Nineteen of them, towards the sea. Had they gone on, into the waves, they'd have got . . . wet.

Said the seventh: Had we gone on, into the sea, we'd have got wet. Had we gone on going on we might easily have got worse than wet. Pneumonia. All kinds of things. You never know, you can't always tell in advance, and to anticipate is only a form of speculation. The seventh policeman hadn't spoken previously. Now he had made up for his earlier silence. He thought of himself as something of an intellectual, a philosopher as well. This because a superior officer had once told him he was.

And the ninth, who quite probably had heard the

seventh, said: And if we – any of us, some of us, all of us – had gone on, out and farther out, we'd either have drowned or have left the ground, risen, floated, swum –

Those of us who could swim, said one of the nineteen, not the ninth, and the voice not easily located. There were nineteen policemen, a total of nineteen, and only their back views were visible.

The Solent shore on Hill Head, Hampshire, 22 July 1974.

We wouldn't do this normally, not for anyone, said the sixth.

It's not normal this, said the twelfth. It doesn't often happen this way. You must admit that.

It isn't – said the third.

Wasn't – said the fifth.

Fucking usual, said the third.

A bus, the silhouette of a bus, on the headland to the east. The fourth remembered that, and commented on it.

At what time? said the tenth.

Then the fourth wondered whether he had remembered it, or was it his imagination at work, deceptive and misleading games being played. Did I comment upon it aloud? Would any of the others have heard me? Was the observation (if such it was) taken down, recorded?

At what time? said the tenth.

What? The fourth was jumpy, nervous.

At what time was the bus? When did you hear it? See it approach?

Oh, when we were walking towards the sea, searching. Searching the shore for . . .

Yes?

You know what. But it's unimportant, I'm certain it is. It couldn't be a clue. I'm sorry I mentioned it.

The bus came and went? The tenth seemed determined

to satisfy himself on the subject.

Oh no. Not that I saw. I didn't see it arrive, or depart. It just happened to be there when I looked up. I looked up and saw it. But it's unimportant.

Don't be afraid to mention anything. Anything, the most unlikely thing, may be the clue for which we're looking, for which you're looking. At any time, in any case. The fourth recollected that the other eighteen had said this in unison, a Greek chorus translated to the Solent shore.

They walked towards the sea.

We walked towards the sea, said the tenth, checking every millimetre of the foreshore. We'd been looking, searching farther up the shore but he probably would have thrown it –

No, buried it –

But it might have been unearthed.

He'd have buried it deep.

If at all.

In the mire. The mud. The sand, earth, silt, sludge – that doesn't matter.

Whatever the substance was.

Dug a deep, deep hole.

We should have brought dogs.

Bulldozers, more likely.

We'll never find it.

Pessimist.

Well, we didn't find it, did we?

Not yet, but patience counts for . . . a great deal, said the seventh.

He'd know, of course, that a found finger-print – a single, solitary, lonely finger-print – would be the end of it.

Of him, you mean.

Who spoke these words was not important. What matters – now – is what was said then, at the time. By one or another of the nineteen.

Good men. And true.

We were, and still are, said one, and a few of the others bothered to laugh.

Policemen searching the Solent shore on 22 July 1974, for a gun.

All the time we knew what we were looking for, said the sixth. Naturally we did. Otherwise, there would have been no point.

We'd been given a detailed description of it the day before. We'd memorized it. What it looked like. The serial number. An obsession in our minds.

We'd been assembled together in this room. A routine briefing session, so we'd thought. The room like a classroom. The nearest thing to one in the building. It served the purpose.

It hadn't been built as a police station, you understand. Not purpose built. It had been designed for other uses.

But it served the purpose. Even a blackboard, and desks, and chalk.

Said the fifth: my throat still remembers the chalk.

We all reported at the same time. So many hundred hours.

Answered our names. Numbers. Ranks.

Sat there.

Or stood.

Each man as he chose.

Not like the good old days when orders were orders and no one used his initiative. Today imagination is brought into play. Each man is encouraged to use his as much as he is able to, to make the most of the grey matter with which he's been born.

Or aspired to.

Had thrust upon him, said the second.

No one laughed. Sometimes such remarks are funny. At other times the same remarks are not funny. Depending on circumstances, depending on all kinds of things.

A sound, a noise. Suddenly.

What was that? said the sixth.

Then there was a laugh, a solitary laugh, from one of his colleagues, police constable someone or other up the line.

A bird, a curlew. Something of the sort.

A naturalist! Well, well. Didn't know you knew the different kinds of feathered friends. Quite the expert.

Leave him alone, said the fifteenth.

There was menace, a little anxiety in the air. Then the sound of the bird again, a cry, a call. No one commented on it this time.

Keep our specialist knowledge to ourselves, don't we? All of us. Unless it's called for, specifically. I wasn't bragging.

Not much to brag about.

Oh, shut up.

Couldn't agree more.

Nineteen policemen searching the Solent shore at Hill Head, Hampshire, on 22 July 1974. For a gun. Those are the bare facts, the bones of the case. An event, you understand, in the past. The date confirms that. It is a date, factual or fictitious, real or invented for present purposes, that has – in reality – taken place. Occurred. Therefore is not happening now, at this moment, as these words proceed, as they are written, as you read them. This, these words, must be some kind of assemblage, a pastiche of reality, or – as the events did take place – a reconstruction.

Nineteen policemen walking towards the sea, our eyes to the ground, searching, searching, seeking, seeking, missing none of the shore, wet or dry, immediately in front of us. This is our voice, our collective voice, our words.

All here?

Number. One two three four . . .

And on to nineteen, the last two in white polo-necked sweaters.

For reasons best known to themselves.

At a later date I told another officer. Someone with whom I was posted. He'd seen, or been told about, the photograph in the paper.

Did you speak to one another?

What, while we were searching? While our eyes were glued, drugged to the ground?

Yes.

I paused for memory, not wanting to be untruthful. It's a funny thing, I said, number twelve said. You know I can't remember, I cannot remember. Even funnier, in a way, I can't remember who was with me.

But weren't there . . . a lot of you?

Nineteen in all, including me. I remember that.

You must know some of them, a few. Surely? You must remember . . . at least one. Is my face not familiar?

I tell you, and if you had been there you would know, we weren't looking at faces. It wasn't like that, not at all. Nothing to do with people we knew, personalities, characters. But we had a common bond.

I was with you.

We were searching for a gun.

I was with you. We were shown it beforehand. The day before.

The gun for which we searched.

If you were shown it, there was no reason for your search.

Our search. You say you were one of us.

No need for our day by the seaside.

Pictures, photos, diagrams, drawings, cross sections. And one like it. Same make, different serial number. A real gun, I mean. A replica. Might have been it, except that it hadn't fired the shots, hadn't his prints upon it.

That we knew because it hadn't fired the shots?

I thought about that, smiled a little at the lips. The image of sticky, hot blood sliding out of the side of my mouth, down my chin, on to my jacket, forced itself into my mind. Identification with the victim? But why at that moment? That we knew because it hadn't fired the shots. Yes, he was right. I said so. No harm in admitting something like that in such a situation. Yes, that's right. I said.

It was, I suppose, from an armoury somewhere, most probably one of ours. Didn't ask, no one did. Not during the briefing. But we knew what we were looking for, what the gun looked like. And we had its serial number.

What kind of gun was it?

I smiled. Of course I can't tell you that.

None of us can.

We were both there. All there.

Sworn to secrecy?

Not exactly that, but there are certain things in the course of one's professional life that one learns not to communicate. Not to communicate to others, I mean. You know that at least as well as I do.

Until the case is closed.

Sometimes not even then. It might, in retrospect, alter the conclusion, the verdict even.

Society has to continue, and continue to function.

There was a pause. The remark, which perhaps had been the intention, had terminated the exchange.

The sound of the sea, washing and rewashing the shore, as if each time it made it dirtier; the sound of feet, policemen's boots; the sound of birds, and of wind.

Searching the Solent shore –

No matter where it was –

For the gun –

You still won't reveal what kind it was? –

Used to kill –

Guns are traditionally used to kill –

Police Constable John Schofield at Caterham on 6 July 1974.

A policeman? Now that puts a different light on matters.

You knew it was a policeman.

May have done, I grant you, may have done, but it does put a different light on things.

In what sense?

Well, I mean. Like one of the family. Keeping it to yourselves. Private grief, like.

He left a wife. And children. You knew that?

We all have wives and children. Some of us, at any rate. It strikes home. Makes it more personal. Could have been any of us.

Exactly. Precisely.

Most people killed must have families. Relatives. Friends. What's the difference; the uniform?

Do I detect in your voice a note of superiority, or cynicism?

Would the search have been less thorough, or more so, had the dead man not been a policeman?

It would have made no difference whatsoever. How could it have done? He had been killed. Someone had shot him. Our job –

Yes, quite.

He had been killed. With a gun. Someone had shot him.

In cold blood.

Hot blood, more likely. Hot, boiling blood.

A pathologist, I see. Welcome to the ranks.

He was killed doing his duty.

There'll be a medal for someone. The widow. At least a commendation.

The shore, the sea, the noise of both. Even in memory they wouldn't die down, cease to have being.

Nineteen men, walking towards the sea, nineteen men who were, who happened to be, policemen. They peered at the foreshore, searching, seeking. For evidence.

For a gun. The gun. Say it, say it.

I'm not afraid to say it. Is that what you think? It's been said.

One of us sighted it, after hours of searching, so it seemed. After hours of walking in file, in line towards the whispering, whistling waves.

Looked up, I did, suddenly, unexpectedly. Hadn't meant to, not premeditated. For no particular reason. Something, a flick of light, must have arrested my attention.

You're a hero.

Ha, ha.

In the sea, the waves, the surface of the water. Maybe it was being swept in, or out.

Did you think that at the time?

I can't say that I did, your Honour. I wouldn't swear to it in the witness box. I wrote nothing in my book, made no note at the time. Or afterwards.

A mirage?

Oh no sir, no.

Go on.

It was a . . . quartz, a piece of stone, flint, a fragment of glass, a side of a plastic cup, a bit of silver chocolate paper, a speck of sand. Water, it could have been the effect of sun on a drop of water. I wouldn't have been the only one to see it. Couldn't have been.

Is that confirmed?

It's not denied.

The tide was . . . going out?

It was a dull day. The water was . . . slow, wherever it was going.

Whether or not it was hiding a gun.

I thought: funny, water is thinner than blood. For some reason that struck me, if you'll pardon the four-letter word, as bloody hilarious. Water is thinner than blood, and the gun could be in the sea.

But the finger-prints wouldn't have been rubbed out by the sea water?

Had the gun been there, bucking in the waves. No.

But the gun wasn't there?

I told you, not that we could discover. There were nineteen of us. It was glass or stone or water. A flash of light, said the first.

I think we've been through that, yes, yes.

All the time we were looking at the ground in front of us. Below us, at our feet. Said the second.

We had our orders. Said the third. We knew what we had to do. What was expected of us, to achieve results. We aren't amateurs, you know.

We searched the ground, and a few inches – two feet even some of the time, when we spread out a little – to left and to right, said the fourth.

X-ray eyes somebody's got. Said the fifth.

Well, they had, hadn't they? said the fourth.

Not as it turned out, that I do admit, said the fifth.

Concession?

Confession.

Eyes in our ears, not to mention our arses, said the sixth.

Naughty. Said the first.

The second was still considering an earlier question. The question was repeated: The tide was going out?

When you're there, on the shore, close enough to inhale the salt and sea smells, the breath of the wind, you don't notice, I do assure you, the direction in which the tide is proceeding.

If proceed, not recede, is the word.

A joke, a joke.

You get on with the job in hand.

Thank you, Officer.

I was wearing dark glasses, said the seventh. But none of the others could see the relevance of the comment.

Not even true, said one.

How do you know? said another. Were you peeping along the line?

No, No. His response was nervous.

Well, then?

I withdraw the remark. Permission to have it removed from the record?

Permission granted.

The day was bleak, grey, static.

Windy?

Cold enough. Whether morning or afternoon, whatever hour or hours. 22 July 1974. A twenty-four-hour period. That much is documented, pinned down. A calendar time.

He was killed on 6 July, sixteen days before the search took place, said the eighth, hands in his trouser pockets, eyes locked to the ground more than five feet below him.

Sixteen days before. The gun could be anywhere. The murderer must be somewhere.

The sea will have passed over the gun tens of times, dozens of times, said the ninth. If it is here at all, that is. If it ever was here.

Why should we assume it was buried here immediately afterwards? said the tenth.

Or at all. Said the eleventh.

There's no point in looking up at the sky. It won't be hanging there from a golden thread, said the third, sarcastically.

We have to look somewhere, said the twelfth, realizing before he had completed his sentence that it wasn't a particularly wise comment. Our superiors, continued the twelfth, who directed us to this beach will have had their reasons.

There are always reasons, said the eleventh. Oh yes, yes.

A seagull swooped, glided parallel to the beach for twenty or thirty yards, then spun away to sea.

Eventually, they stopped, the nineteen men, the nineteen policemen. They stopped walking towards the sea. At some point, some time, they had to turn back. They had to return to the station, and afterwards to their homes, their wives and children if they had them, or wherever they went at the end of the day's work. The sea was grey, out at sea, in the deep, towards the horizon. Horizon? A seamless join where somewhere sea and sky collided. No indication of where one began, the other ended. Only sounds of the sea shore, not sights.

The thirteenth looked up, ahead of him, but neither observed nor intended to observe what was in front. He was thoughtful.

Funny if he was behind us, watching us. He said.

Who? said the man next to him, the fourteenth, looking round slightly so as to see the profile of the thirteenth.

Him. Said the thirteenth, certain it was obvious whom he meant, without having to spell it out, to name the name. Not the christened, baptized, given name – if they had known that, could they have known that, how much less difficult would everything have been – but the man's role. They knew it was a man. There are some things where certainty is absolute.

The murderer. He said.

What? Behind us? Said the fifteenth. You're joking, must be. I hope.

He hasn't seen our faces. He doesn't know which of us . . . what we look like. We haven't looked up. Not since we came here. And certainly not behind us.

But when did he start to follow us? said the sixteenth.

If he's behind us, my friend. If he's behind us. I didn't say more than that. Said the thirteenth.

We don't want identi-kit pictures in every newspaper. That would confuse the issue. Everyone would look like everyone else. Everyone would be suspicious of everyone else. Said the seventh, but somehow utterly lacking conviction in what he said. Did he feel that the others would sense his lack of belief in his own pronouncements?

We had to turn round some time, said the seventeenth. The sea would come in, the waters rise right up the shore, way beyond us and past us, up to the line of seaweed there. If we remained where we were, we'd be submerged, obliterated, even those of us over six feet three inches, and I'm not that high.

The bus.

Ah, the bus. Had we forgotten the bus?

No, it had no further part to play. It had been altogether an irrelevance, a red herring.

The cries of the sea birds. The sheer pressure, the intensity of the sounds and life of the sea, the iceberg-like coming together of the swell of water, a packing of power, of water slapping, slapping the shore, erasing all clues of the previous moment and before. The vastness of the two blues, the two greys, sky and wet, become one. The tang of a hidden, secret world beneath and within the spatial landscape. Seascape. Beachscape.

If he's behind us, said the eighteenth. If he's behind us, he's probably, almost definitely, holding a gun.

The gun.

The murder weapon. Aiming it at us.

At one of us. Said the nineteenth. The odds against it being you or me, any one of us, are pretty high.

You find that a consolation? said the seventh.

The question was left unanswered, allowed to remain a question. An answer had been expected. It was not meant to be rhetorical.

It's time, said the first.

Time? said the third.

And the first: The end, the end of the day. The light's going, too. It's time.

Saw them, nineteen of them, eyes to the ground, looking for the gun used to kill. A policeman. Solidarity, that's what they showed. None of them would be . . . interviewed. None of them would reveal themselves, as individuals. They represented, and represent, law and order. We all pay rates, don't we? They are part of what we buy. Our policemen. Yours, mine. I'd hoped to have obtained nineteen separate accounts from them of their day's activities but, well, I am no tape-recorder, no sociologist. Another time, maybe. The documentation will still be there.

The gun? How did I know they were looking for a

gun? Someone must have told me. If they found it, they didn't say, and I didn't see any of them bend down and reach for it. But they wouldn't have let on, not before the case came to court. Maybe they'll search further. Tomorrow, or the day after, or the day after that.

HIGH AND LIFTED UP

KIRKPATRICK DOBIE

THIS YEAR we went to Troon. My wife preferred Ayr but I held out for Troon and got my way. It was selfish, for Ayr is a better place for shopping and I could easily have travelled to Troon for golf. This was pointed out but I said the converse also was true: that she could travel from Troon for shopping and have her unselfishness as a bonus.

It is seldom I assert myself like this but when I do, I am like Toad in *The Wind in the Willows*, I have the gift of words. I have always had it and it has never done me any good. I knew that, but I didn't want to go to Ayr. I hadn't seen the town for years and had, I had thought, almost forgotten, but as soon as it was mentioned I knew I couldn't go. So we went to Troon and I played golf while my wife took the children to Ayr and Afflecks and shopped and gave them ice-cream in the cafeteria. Sometimes, of course, we were all together and she and I sat on the beach while they played and paddled and made sandcastles, but when we did, it was at Troon.

The house in Ayr had been number twenty-two Alexandria Terrace, a bungalow in a row of bungalows, and you can tell the sort of bungalow it was from the fact it had a number and not a name. There my mother and

I had stayed for a month with its owner Mrs McKinnon, and her daughter Bella. I knew Mrs McKinnon was owner for she was forever saying: 'At least I've always the hoose.' She had said it as if deprived, or expecting to be deprived, of everything else. She was a thin frizzy-haired woman with a Glasgow accent and an expression of alarmed concern. I remember her perfectly but she does not stand out in any way. I think it is because she was so ordinary. She was like her bungalow – anonymous.

But if Mrs McKinnon was ordinary the same could not be said of Bella. I suppose 'Bella', so seeming-Scots, is really from Italian – beautiful, and that is what Bella was. She was beautiful and even at ten I knew it. Where she got her looks I didn't know. I decided it was from her absent father, for I was much given to speculation – a precocious, sickly child. For some reason I assumed he was a sailor. I learned afterwards he was a solicitor's clerk who had run off with another woman.

Looking back, I can see I was wrong thinking Bella's looks came from her father. Mrs McKinnon was ordinary only because she was elderly and defeated. Even so, had a wealthy half-remembered uncle died – say in Australia – leaving her a fortune, or had she had a big win on the Pools – or rather, on the Calcutta Sweepstake, for there were no Pools in those days – had either of these things happened, and as a result, had some presentable widower or middle-aged bachelor begun to pay her attention, which in the circumstances might well have been the case, then I think Mrs McKinnon would have looked very well. She might, indeed, have looked pretty, for when I thought of it, I could recall in her not one bad feature, and her figure, though perhaps a little drooped, was still, especially when viewed from behind, almost girlish.

However, I had no eyes for Mrs McKinnon or anyone

else when Bella was around. She was good-natured as well as beautiful, though perhaps it was I who brought that out, for I think she must have been flattered by my attention. She ought to have been, for a child's response to beauty is out of this world, and, I am inclined to think, one of the few things that suggests a better one. It is so innocent and absolute.

Because it was September and the local children all back at school, I had only my mother's company in the early part of the day, but most evenings and on odd afternoons I had Bella's. At nights we played draughts and on afternoons, when my mother took a nap, we went to the beach. Some evenings when she had no other engagement, we went to the cinema.

My mother never accompanied us. She didn't like the beach. It was too blowy for her, and she didn't care for what she called 'the pictures'. They hurt her eyes. Looking back, I can see she was not too pleased about my attachment. I was supposed to be recovering from bronchitis and she made difficulties about the night air. I was forced to wear my scarf and heavy overcoat which was a great inconvenience.

I said we went out when Bella had no other engagement, but her engagements were few. Her boy-friend was a Glasgow doctor who was free only twice a week and that included Sunday afternoons. When he arrived there was a great to-do and Mrs McKinnon prepared special food – steak and chips with fried tomatoes, or salmon and salad and two kinds of bread – white and brown. She exerted herself even to the point of making little jokes, as that John would have to look to his laurels or I would be cutting him out. I think she may even have passed my mother and me off, not as boarders, but friends on a visit.

But I could be wrong. It is only now I think of it.

Bella did not exert herself. Looking back, I believe she thought her mother overdid it, though again I can't recall why I should think so, except that it would be in character. Anyhow, I am certain she was just as she always was, and as her mother was never. She was perfectly natural and light-hearted but no more than usual.

When John came I ceased to be the centre of things and might have been expected to resent this but I didn't. I rather liked him. Or at least, I approved him. He was, I suppose, under thirty, but seemed to me older, burly, with crisp black hair and a thoughtful, almost brooding expression. He looked to me a very sound, deliberate, sort of man, and though clearly far older, quite the right sort for Bella.

I suppose I thought he was the right sort because some part of my feeling for her was protective. I don't know why. She was about nineteen and there was nothing in her to suggest helplessness. Her mother had a helpless, not to say hopeless, air, but not Bella. She was always sweet and gay. All the same, when we went to the cinema, in spite of my restrictive overcoat, woolly scarf, and flat cap – the last, with my head in it, reaching not quite up to her shoulder – in spite of all that, I felt myself in charge. I felt responsible for her.

One night coming home – it was just after nine, for of course, we went to the early house – she asked if I liked John.

'Yes,' I said. Until then, I hadn't thought, but when I did, I saw it was roughly expressive of what I felt.

'Do *you?*' I asked. It was a silly question, but after the manner of children I asked again, and when she didn't answer, kept repeating it till we had left the traffic and passed into quieter ways. Then she said: 'I love him.'

I took that in my stride because at my age, precocious though I was, I didn't know what it meant.

By the end of three weeks my holiday had done me so much good that I prevailed on my mother to extend it. She was easily won by appeals to considerations of health for she was perhaps a little hypochondriac. So, at the expense of my schooling, we stayed.

I never knew what Bella did for a living. I never thought of it. I think I imagined vaguely that she worked in an office, though in imagination I could never place her in one. In imagination I saw her always on the shore, her hair blown, or head bent over the draught-board in the gas-light. I think her hair had some kind of kink in it that made me remember. Anyhow, it is clear to me now, in this present time, that she must have worked in a shop or possibly a café, otherwise she would have been free on Saturdays and never on odd afternoons. Today, I expect, it would have been hairdressing. One of those expensive establishments staffed by lovely but unclever girls, who do something of fleeting effect called permanent waving.

I don't know whether Bella was clever or not. It was not that I was too young to assess; the fact was, I never gave myself a chance. I talked all the time. I was a terribly garrulous little boy and her presence inspired me. It was all I had to give, and I gave her all I had. For all that, I found, and find, her impossible to describe, any more than I can describe the effect she had on me, except that my talking was part of it. Of course, she was beautiful, but who can describe that? I think she walked well – I mean moved well – but it was unstudied. She did not present or impose herself. She did not, I think, initiate anything. It was rather that she was responsive, and made me think well of myself as well as of her. She may, after all, have been clever, and that may have been part of it. I don't know. I don't suppose it matters.

The days slid into one another and passed until the last but one was reached. It was a Friday and when it came the sky was overcast. By the afternoon it looked like rain but with a rising wind that I persuaded my mother would keep the rain away, and so, and because it would be for the last time, I was allowed to go out.

We went first by the foreshore and then to the headland, a direction we had never taken before. I thought it would be great to see the breakers sweep under the cliffs, 'tossing their shaggy manes' I said, for I was much given to phrase-making and phrase-quoting. At the back of my mind, too, had been the idea the cliffs would be deserted and I should have her to myself this last afternoon and that it would be so much the more prolonged.

It was still unwet when we reached the top, and there the wind blew with tremendous strength, summoning itself for great gusts 'like an enormous cornet player' I would have told her, but could not make myself heard. We joined hands and were swept along, my coat billowing, my scarf a pennon, while far below the waves mounted, jostled, sloshed, and disappeared, and came endlessly on again.

We were quite safe. The path had a parapet and there was no danger. It was all to be enjoyed and presently the sun struggled forth and from violet blackness the waves came crested like gleaming lances in a torchlight procession. I was exhilarated and afraid. It was a fearful joy.

What followed remains unclear: I think she stopped and

we held together, and I think she would have stayed but the wind was too much. We were whirled away. We ran and ran, and Bella ran so wildly and held me so hard that we went in circles. I was lifted up, I was wine swirled in a wine glass. Then we crashed and she lay, face leaden, eyes open, staring up and beyond me.

I found myself crying and pulling at her arm and at last got her to her feet. I was unhurt and after a bit I retrieved her hat. It was a red Tam o' Shanter and she beat it against her knee, but her hands shook so much she could scarcely put it on. I think she tried to say something but if she did the wind carried it away. I thought she wanted to go back, but at last I understood she was afraid.

We took a path at right angles to the shore and must have been an odd-looking pair, she so sagged and beautiful and I, small and chunky on thin shanks, taking as much of her weight as I could. It was a long journey, and to make matters worse it began to rain, not heavily, but driving with all the force of the wind. About half way, we stopped at a corrugated-iron shelter. There we huddled and she was so wan and weak I felt myself dissolved. It was quite extraordinary, for talking apart, I was not a demonstrative child, and am not, even now, a demonstrative man, but I put my arms about her and kissed her. I kissed her gently again and again. It seemed, at the time, quite natural. I did not ask any questions or even speak, and that was extraordinary too. I just sat there holding her and saying nothing.

When we got back, Mrs McKinnon was at the front door peering up and down the road. 'Whaur hae ye been?' she said. 'Your mother's awa doon the front wi' her umbrella. She thinks ye're blawn ower the cliffs.' And she added something to the effect that I would have lost 'a' the guid o' ma holiday'.

But it was Bella who did not appear for supper and I never saw her again. Next day was Saturday and she was off to work before I was out of bed. John came in the afternoon. There was a football match he wanted to see and he took me with him. He was, as I said, rather a nice man, and he paid my threepence at the turnstile. That's all it was in those days – a long time ago. At some point in the course of the game I told him everything – or nearly everything. I couldn't help it. It just came out. I was so sadly concerned and so cursedly talkative. He listened, not making much of it, but not interrupting. He was very sensible and he was a doctor. I suppose I thought he was to be trusted. But even then, in my youth and weakness, I knew I was betraying her.

It seems incredible after all these years, a thing like that, though important enough at the time, should divert me – and of course, my wife and family – to Troon. But there it was. I suppose I never really got over Bella. Had we gone to Ayr, I think I should almost certainly have found myself one morning – or afternoon – or evening – at number twenty-two Alexandria Terrace, waiting, having rung the bell. Bella would be now over forty, an epileptic, perhaps a spinster. I could hear myself saying: 'Mrs McKinnon?' and then realizing.

CALL ME

NAOMI MITCHISON

I DID at last inherit the dolls' house. I had wanted it all along, but my Grannie passed it on to Aunt Mima and trust her not to give me a thought, though I daresay she never-ever turned the key in the lock. Oh, it was locked right enough in her house, though it had been often enough opened for me in Grannie's day. Poor Grannie, she lived in one of the top flats in Buccleuch Place and a great view out of the back windows, but awkward with her getting old and needing to cry down to the lower flat to bring up her milk and her loaf. I was in Aberdeen at the time and my eldest not walking yet, or I'd have come more often. But when I was a wee one myself she was bright and bustling, the china all washed to a sparkle, and a tea caddy on the middle table that had pan-drops in it, or else Berwick cockles, and Grannie wasn't sparing of them.

I'd be sucking away and then she'd turn the brass key in the front of the dolls' house. But there was always one thing that I couldn't get out of my mind. That was the differences in sizes of the furniture. The bedroom furniture was for someone quite wee; there was a small brass bed with a silk quilt and a chest of drawers that pulled out; one could put things into it like – I remember – a squashed daisy that I'd laid into my prayer book from the edge of the kirk path. I was taken to the kirk in those days, Sabbath by Sabbath, which is maybe why I cannot care for it now.

Then there was a dressing table that opened out, with a scrap of a blotted mirror inside that one could make stand up and a tiny pair of scissors, and spaces for other things which had been lost over the years, but I never could make up my mind what they could be. There was what she'd call a chaise percée in ivory with a tiny silver chamber pot in it, a brown and white hip bath with a soap dish, and a hanging cupboard with a coloured picture on the door, but that, she'd tell me, was from her own days. So much of the rest was old, old, and I would think now that it could have come from a time when the family was up in the world. Not that we are down now, no such thing, but we would neither afford nor approve the kind of unpractical life that folk led them. Dolls' furnishings in ivory and silver indeed! Yet I liked them.

But I am getting away from the dolls' house bedroom; the other thing it had was a trimmed rocking cot with a baby in it. Well, all that fitted fine with the doll lady who sometimes stood by the dressing table, but was sometimes put to bed with her silk dress off and wearing only a chemise of thin lawn which had been darned in two places, long ago. But the school-room had bigger furniture with bamboo frames, a painted table, and a globe that could scarcely have been moved by the bedroom lady. It had pictures on the walls, crochet rugs and some miniature books, though one was a Koran, and as soon as I got round to knowing what it was, I was dead sure nobody would have taught Arabic to the dolls' house children.

But the drawing-room was bigger in scale yet; it had a

set of dark wood furniture, intricately carved, from Goa, my Grannie said, and bye and bye I looked it up in my school atlas. The bedroom lady could barely have peeped over the top of the table or lifted a cup of the flowered tea set which was laid out on it. There were glass vases too, and cushions the right size for the Goan chairs. There was a swinging glass bird cage with a bright glass bird inside it. Best of all there was a silver teapot and a pair of candle-sticks that Grannie kept polished, and a gilt clock with tiny statuettes, one on each side. Once when I was a child I put in what was clearly meant as a smart electric standard lamp with a pink silk shade which had been given me on a birthday; it seems to me now that it was a great kindness in Grannie not to throw the thing out, so ill did it go with the rest.

Kitchen and dining-room had mixed sizes. There were all the gay-coloured plaster food dishes, turkeys and hams and sausages, gigots of meat, cakes and oranges, goblets of purple wine that couldn't come out. Here there was a dining table from Goa, the legs and sides darkly carved. The centre-piece was a three-tiered china stand, very pretty, my favourite thing when I was a wee girl, and on the dining-room mantelshelf a carved chamois under branching trees. Swiss, it would have been. Kitchen and tableware were the right size for the bedroom lady and, what was more, the cook with her cap and apron was the right size too. But then there were wooden pails and jugs and a churn, from Germany I think, and meant for someone bigger. And there was a pussycat in a basket which was almost tiger size but luckily sound asleep. Once, said Grannie, there had been a gentleman, her husband, and a little girl in pantalettes. But they were gone.

Whenever I got the lady out of bed she had to go right down to the kitchen to consult with the cook among the pans and the kettles and the girdle that were the right size for them both. The lady had a mauve and green dress and tiny black boots painted on to her china feet. I remembered the pattern all my days. Grannie said she was called Lady Mousiekin, but the cook was just plain Bella. The lady's husband was called Sir Ranald Mousiekin. 'Did he wear a kilt?' I asked.

'No, my dear,' said Grannie, 'a kilt looks badly on a doll, just the same as a lassie looks badly dancing the fling. Sir Ranald wore the dress uniform of an officer, tartan trews, a well-fitting jacket and a small sword. There was a gillie too, with big whiskers. But some way, while I was growing up, those two disappeared, and the young daughter as well. Someone must have taken them.'

'But who could it have been?' I asked. It was such a sad thing!

'Nobody could say and they told me I was too old to play with a dolls' house.'

'I'll never be too old, Grannie!' I said. I kept on asking questions. Grannie didn't know the baby's name, but I called him Wee Dougal; he hadn't much of a face and was all wrapped up. I didn't care to unwrap him because he mightn't have had a body.

And there they stayed, shut in, all the time Aunt Mima had the dolls' house, up in that top attic in Morningside. She'd had a sad life and wasn't tired speaking of it. It seems she had been engaged to be married in 1914 when she was a young girl, but he had been killed. He was in the Black Watch and Aunt Mima still had cuttings about the battle of Richebourg L'Avoué, yellowed pieces from *The Scotsman* and then, the casualty lists and his name ringed in black. I hated seeing that and if she showed it me once she showed it a dozen times. After she died I found all those bits of paper and his photo, and some old letters stamped 'Passed by the Censor', from him no doubt, all tied up with ribbon; I burnt them at once. Why couldn't she have let me have the dolls' house, me with a young family, though it's a fact they were boys and mightn't have appreciated it? But no. If I'd had a wee girl, she said. But it was I myself wanting the dolls' house. I dreamed of it sometimes.

Of course Grannie was almost bound to have left it, with the rest of her good furniture, to Aunt Mima who was her daughter. It would have looked queer leaving it to my father and I doubt Grannie would never have skipped a generation with anything big, though she did leave me her garnet necklace and ear-rings, not that I ever wear them. But some way it seemed hardly fair, Aunt Mima keeping it shut all those years; she didn't even want me to see it when I came over, as I did a couple of times in the year, oftener even, as she grew older – and worse tempered. And then she died and there was nobody else to leave it to. Or so I felt.

Well now, the first thing I did was to open all the drawers and take the lids off everything and give it all a good dusting. I couldn't find the big ashet with the two chickens and when I opened the dressing table the scissors were gone. Oh, I was that cross! There was a chip off the china centre-piece in the dining-room and of course she'd never bothered to polish the wee teapot and the candlesticks, as I did, the very first thing. But then, in the drawer of the kitchen dresser under the soup ladle, there was this paper and all it said was Call Me. It was written small in brownish ink and in a hand I didn't know. But what could it mean? I was fairly puzzled by this for I knew well enough it had not been there when I played with the dolls' house last. Yes, I puzzled my head. Who wouldn't?

Call me. You'd think I could have laid it by, just an old scrap of paper out of a dolls' house, but some way I couldn't. I felt a need to call – someone. I have never in my life been scared of ghosts and bogles and such; that was something which had passed me by altogether, even when I was a wee child. But I thought, well, whoever it is, I'll not call *her*. Aunt Mima was bad enough in real life. But I called softly Grannie, Grannie. I'd never-ever have been scared of her, even if she'd come back in a shroud. She'd still pet me up and give me pan-drops and laugh with me. But there was no answer, not even a shiver.

I began to shift the furniture in the dolls' house. You know, I had never asked which of the family had been to Goa; I just took it for granted. Once, later on, I had asked my father, but he had no idea and was not interested. It came to my mind suddenly that I ought to call whoever it was in Goa had made the furniture too big and get him to alter it – such fancies one has! But a person cannot be called without a name to call him by.

So there I was, making up stories to myself, and the boys coming in for their supper. Alastair was at the University by now, but he'd a habit of having one solid meal a day in his home! They'd all been teasing me about the dolls' house and how I'd got it at last. So I wasn't going to speak to those lads about the paper with the writing on it, whoever else I spoke to. I'd the queerest feeling that if I'd had a daughter – but three boys are enough for anyone surely! – I could have told her about it. I'd tears at the back of my eyes over this very thing. I tried to put it out of my mind and when it would not leave me, when it kept jagging at me, I had a wee talk with my husband late in the evening, trying to make light of the paper and how there must be a sensible explanation. He was quite concerned but said to me that I should throw the piece of paper into the back of the fire. 'I'll do just that,' I said, and indeed I meant it, but the sitting-room fire was out and we were in our beds and tomorrow would be time enough. He said, too, that he himself with such a problem, would find help in reading the Book. But he knew well enough that I was not that way given. Yet, out of fondness, I promised that I would do that as well the next morning.

But tomorrow came and it seemed to me stupid to go to the lengths of burning the paper; that was like something in a cheap film. In real life one just laughs at oneself and forgets all about it. Only that was not how it was working out. I felt a great curiosity growing in me, I just had to know who was to be called – and why. So when the house was empty I went back up to the dolls' house and I got myself a cushion and sat down on the floor and called by name every one of the dolls: the two who were there and the lost husband and child and gillie. I even called the baby in the cot. But what I'd have done if there had been an answer is beyond me. There was none of course, but if there had been would I have kept my head or would I have been scared and bolted back downstairs and rung up my husband's office, though he never likes me to do that? Or what?

And I kept on puzzling: why in the kitchen dresser? When was it put there? Was it some kind of revenge by Aunt Mima because I had a husband and children and she had none? But I knew her handwriting and it did not match up with this. The paper looked as if it had been cut along the edges; could she have found it in an old letter and cut it out and laid it there? A crazy idea and

I knew it, but I could get nothing to fit and the afternoon was wearing on and it darted across my mind that it could have been in a letter from that laddie who was killed in 1915. But was it his handwriting, and, if so, had Aunt Mima, once upon a time, called him and he had not come? For if he had she would have been different. Somehow I knew that. And besides this was nonsense. I knew I had burned his letters, all, all, so I could not compare the writing, and I began to feel a grey sadness pressing me down, a kind of guilt, and with it a strong determination that I would never, never, call Aunt Mima.

Did I read a chapter in the Book? I did not. That too seemed to me not just genuine, in spite of my husband truly thinking it could help me. My Grannie could have got comfort from the Book; I remembered how she'd had bookmarks with flowers painted on them to mark the pages she liked best. But today's world is different. I wondered if Aunt Mima had been helped at all by that kind of reading, but I thought not. I thought her pain had to be borne without this sort of poultice. Nor could it affect my own trouble, which was not pain or loss but an anxiety which I could not quite pin down.

How did it end? Ah, there, I'm afraid you have me. For it has not ended. I put back the piece of paper and shut the drawer and made myself a good strong cup of tea to bring me back to my right senses. And now there grew up in me a determination to put back the piece of paper and shut the drawer for all the rest of my life, but I would put more than the soup ladle on the top of it. I went out and bought a piece of good white material and I hemmed it round into three table cloths to fit the dining-room table, each with an initial M for Mousiekin embroidered in the corner. I put the iron over them and now they are folded up neatly in the drawer on the top of the paper, with the soup ladle above them, and there they will stay.

I like to show my old dolls' house to visitors and I can tell you, I was just delighted when Alastair's girl-friend came in one evening and asked to see it. In no time she was looking at everything, picking out the prettiest, asking could she make some small re-arrangements and promising me that she'd somehow find a doll the right size for Lady Mousiekin and with the same kind of china face. She'd look in one or two of the old shops along the High Street, she said, and when Alastair started to laugh it was she who shut him up. She'd another notion which I find myself taken with : that she should try for a doll the right size for the big furniture.

'We could even,' she said – and I liked the way she'd said 'we', yes, I thought it boded well – 'have an Indian doll, to go with those chairs from Goa, a lady in a lovely sari. How would you like that?'

'I think it would be right,' I said, 'but they could never meet, could they now?'

'No, no,' she said, 'we'll keep them apart. It will just mean a trifle of re-organization.'

Of course she and Alastair are not exactly engaged; that would be too old-fashioned for them. But I wouldn't wonder if the next thing might be a wedding, even if it is not the kind of good-going wedding that we had in our day with a fine cake and a sit-down tea and photographers and plenty of drink but not too much. No, they'd do it their own way and doubtless for a while they'd both be working. But later on, they might have a wee girl. Yes, like I was once myself.

And then I could leave the dolls' house to her, and she

would be certain sure to open all the drawers and she would find the paper and read it. And who would she call? Never Aunt Mima; for she is deader than the dolls. Her name will have been forgotten, only something on the flyleaf of a few old books. No, my grand-daughter will never call that one. But who will she call? Maybe me.

THE CLOWN AS LOVER

ARTHUR YOUNG

WHEN I was a young man all my attempts at love left me humiliated and hurt. In time I came to accept that my short legs, my rotund figure, and the early loss of hair, were grave handicaps in this area of human experience.

Since, however, I am by nature passionate and sensuous, I had to find some way of matching my desires to my physical failings. Having come to disbelieve in the emotion of love and having no confidence in my ability to attract I decided to take the safe way out: I would buy my favours.

To begin with I tried the obvious, the commercial market.

In my first untutored episode I lost wallet, skin and dignity. From then I avoided like the plague the girls of ponces. I then took up with an obliging lady whom I met in a lounge bar drinking vodka and tonic water: but she perspired and tended to slip from under. By mistake I petitioned one of perverse proclivity: but her curious postures aroused no response in me. I surrendered to the expert eurythmics of a call girl from Manchester: but her mechanical oscillations left me unmoved.

I reconsidered the situation.

After some time I tried another seam, a more respectable stratum. This I have found richly rewarding.

Here I found widows over the shock of grief and now without the comfortable release of married life; older girls aching for masculine smells and company, but imprisoned by ailing mothers; executive ladies who had looked up from their careers too late.

They accepted my buffoon's figure to provide the semblance of love. I replied with courtesy, sympathy and a deference to their womanhood.

Since, like me, they had accepted disappointment and came to these affairs with no expectation beyond physical relief, the reaction to such considerations produced a glow of friendliness and a mutual respect which, if not the heights of love, at least lifted these encounters from the sordid and left the agonists some self-pride.

Of course sensibilities are delicate at such times. The matter of tribute is one of subtlety.

I pride myself that I have developed a flair for sensing the right moment, the proper gesture.

It is often no more than a good meal with life viewed for an hour or so through the ruby shade of a good claret. I have known it be a companionable walk, window shopping, with the gift of a chance-noticed bauble.

One of my best efforts was with a widow who had four children. We went to a supermarket, the whole bunch of us, and bought enough tins to last six months and enough cornflakes to feed a horse.

All of the kids had trolleys. We played at fire engines up and down the aisles; then had ice-creams and cakes and doughnuts at the counter.

Breakfast next morning was a hilarious affair. I announced a morning off school and the children were all over porridge and marmalade. Afterwards I wanted to slip quietly out the back way.

'No!' she said. 'You're a good soul. You leave this house

with my blessing and damn the neighbours.'

She kissed me frankly on the lips at her front gate and the children gave me sticky hugs. They waved until I was out of sight.

I was tempted to turn back. Their tears had been real. But I stuck to my self-made rules. If I never went back I could never be hurt. I could make believe in a sort of love and preserve the memory intact. But I would not risk my comic appearance turning it sour in time.

Strict observance of this precept had been wise. At least so I thought until last summer when I had to go to Sheffield.

I arrived at my hotel late on Sunday afternoon to be ready for a sharp start on Monday. After washing I slept on top of the bed for half an hour. I woke hungry, ready for a drink, and unexpectedly randy. As I went down to the bar and to order dinner, I was not too hopeful of satisfying my third need.

Sunday night in that provincial capital of steel did not seem auspicious for lust. Sensible Yorkshire girls would have Monday morning on their minds and be away home to bed early.

At first sight the field was not promising. A few groups of commercials were swapping stories with guffaws of forced laughter. One or two couples sipped drinks and talked privately. At the back of the room, however, against the wall, a woman sat on her own.

She was neatly dressed, and with some style. She had an uncomplicated whisky pony in front of her. I liked that. Then, too, she looked straight at me: but with neither coyness nor the least hint of come on.

There is nothing to be gained by being devious at such times. I ordered my drink at the bar; paid for it; then took the glass and went straight towards her, ignoring everyone else in the room. I paused briefly:

'May I join you?'

Her reply was easy, direct, and with a little smile.

'Please do!'

I sat down. Anyone watching would have thought the meeting arranged; would have taken the few words for the quiet greetings of acquaintances. Only she and I knew the worlds of commentary in our words, our mutual appraisal.

Long ago I gave up subterfuge. I introduced myself; stated my business; said I would be leaving on Tuesday.

'But I would be glad of your company tonight and tomorrow evening, if you care to join me.'

As I spoke, I took in her figure, no longer hidden by the table. I wondered if I had made a mistake.

Nature had played atrocious tricks with her internal machines. She had been given a gargantuan appetite, but lacked the glandular secretions to burn away the excess.

Although the face was brave and young and the chin had the merest dewlap, from the neck down her flesh strained in mounds and hills and bulges and swells and billows of fat. Because of her youth it was restrained by an elastic skin and kept in some order by young muscles, but the years would bring a melting, a downflowing which would consign her to grotesque corpulence and waddling movements.

As she answered in agreement, her steady gaze measured my reaction to her close up.

Of course, I showed none. My own experience had made me a past master at dissembling; at avoiding hurt.

Her fine eyes held my attention. They bore out my initial judgement. The girl had an ineffable distinction.

Soon I suggested dinner. She agreed avidly; said she

was famished. Once again I admired her directness.

As she preceded me to the dining room I saw that her buttocks were massive, and a slight chiffing noise told that her thighs rubbed together in colossal companionship.

But it was of note that, as she ordered her meal with decision and clarity, she commanded instant civility from the waiter.

As we ate and talked, I marvelled at her build. There was a solidity about the packed flesh that made nothing of her years, for she was but newly twenty. It should have taken a lifetime to achieve such lusty bulk.

Yet her eating gave away the secret. As the food was laid before us there came a glister to her eyes, a wetness to the tongue and lips, the slightest slaver as she talked.

'Food!' she said. And was from then wordless as she tore into it with small voracious bites, demolishing platefuls with brisk knife cuts and quick fork stabs and dexterous spoon dips.

'How does she live, this charming girl, within her fat self?' I wondered. Beside hers, my own problems were insignificant. How sore must her heart have been: and how often.

From her look at that moment, I had a sudden divination that she was likewise remarking on my own absurdities.

We laughed at our unspoken perspicacity.

She came to bed without demur.

While undressing she exhibited a paradox of hippopotamine daintiness as she stepped neatly from her clothes and gracefully divested her body of its ridiculous lingerie.

But, as I might have expected, her personal hygiene was fresh and redolent of past fashions, of lavender and

Pears soap. She disdained to disguise the scent of her approaching excitement with one of those disgusting sprays.

I found this lack of sophistication quite enchanting and we brought to our first corpulent copulation an air which, had I been less experienced, I might easily have taken for romance. The second time brought laughter and relaxation and a return to the mundane.

In the night I woke. I put on the bed light to look at her and to marvel again. I traced my finger between her Buddha breasts and tried to gauge their measure. It would have taken four hands.

She opened her eyes, sleepy at first; then concern showed.

'Is there something wrong?'

'No! No!' I answered gently. 'Everything is as it should be. You go to sleep.'

She fell asleep at once, trusting in my words.

I could not get my arms around her, but nestled into her enfolding flesh. Soon it lay heavily on me. I became cramped and stiff: but not for the world would I have disturbed her.

Next morning she had to leave early for her own work. I lay in the huge hot hollow she had left, enjoying her precise movements as she dressed. We chatted amiably. I probed gently, trying to find something to do that evening; somewhere to go that would please her.

Unexpectedly she said:

'Do you swim?'

I said that I did.

'Come swimming with me then. Five o'clock at the town hall. We could have a picnic afterwards if the evening is fine.'

A picnic! I had not been on one for years. I clapped

my hands at the unexpected delight.

Even as she proposed making sandwiches and taking coffee in a flask I pooh-poohed the idea. My mind ran ahead. Here was my opportunity to show my flair for the gesture judged to a nicety.

She was surprised, but obviously pleased by my enthusiastic response.

That lunchtime I excused myself from my associates and the usual gin-tub business meal. Instead, I paid a visit to the city centre. I bought a raffia basket and in the big market I filled it with delicacies that I thought would tempt her: pâté, chicken, fresh French bread; a bottle of peaches in brandy, cream. To drink I found some Tokay.

In a junk shop off the Moor I happened on a pair of tortoiseshell hair combs set with silver. They would compliment her personal appearance yet without risk of hurt.

Going back to my business conference in the afternoon, I found it difficult to concentrate as a sense of happy anticipation welled up in me. But the thought of the picnic was not my only reason for pleasure. Never before that I could remember had I been able to look forward to showing off before a woman.

I have explained that I am short on the qualities of male display. But in the water my lack of inches is not important. My porpoise figure is indeed an asset.

For, you see, I can swim like a fish.

That evening we met in the town and drove to the Derbyshire hills in the South. Although Sheffield is a city of great and grimy industry it is rich in parks set in the nearby hills.

High above the smoke-wrapped city we swam in the evening sun.

She, too, was expert in the water. Like me she gained a weightlessness when swimming. She had a fast, relaxed crawl and performed with neatness from the springboard. Her massive bulk split the surface with a contained splash and her small feet pointed skywards in taut control.

We raced once or twice, but I beat her easily, even though I gave her a generous handicap. I sunned myself in her praise, a feminine commodity unknown to me. I noticed a deepening interest, an added awareness.

Afterwards the picnic was a great success. She exclaimed in delight as I set it before her on a plaid rug I brought from the car. Each item was received with relish :

'Ooh ! I love those ! Mmm ! Scrumptious !'

And her small mouth smacked and sucked in gustatory anticipation.

I was gratified. Yet for a moment I wished it had not been calculated in past experience; wished it had been innocent; the first time.

Still, the effect was what I had planned.

Afterwards we scrambled to the top of the peak and held hands in out-of-breath wonder.

That night we were tired by the wine, the exercise and the fresh air. We fell asleep not attempting love.

Once more I awoke in the night. Moved by a wish to protect and comfort I grappled to encompass her lumpen body in my arms. But again I could not manage. I finished by cuddling childwise into the bulge of her abdomen.

In the morning she asked, 'Can I see you off ?'

I was touched and agreeably surprised.

'I would like that very much. What about your work ?'

She shrugged.

'I'm never late! They can stand it for once!'

We took a long time to the meal, polishing the detail of our encounter into a bright memory.

Then, to take the hurt from our parting, and because the time seemed right, I made a present of the combs.

For some moments she handled them but said nothing. Then:

'They are exquisite.'

'I'm glad you like them.'

She gave me a direct look which brought blood to my face. I wished it had been the first present I had given any girl.

'Payment?' she asked.

It was a true question. There was no rhetoric in it. No hint of sarcasm. But I realized that on my reply would rest her peace of mind for a long time to come.

Yet I did not have to manufacture a reply. It came without volition, without thought.

'Indeed, no! For love!'

It was the first time I had so used that word.

Her posture slackened a degree as she gave in to this strange truth.

She poured my final cup of coffee, put the combs into her bag with a gentle movement. Then she left.

I left Sheffield and drove north. I headed for Carter Bar and home.

As I drove, however, I owned to myself a bleak misery in which I discerned a fine irony.

At last I was the perfect Clown.

A LASTING IMPRESSION

ANNE TURNER

THE STORM caught them enjoying the slow summer dusk along the shore road. Massing clouds and sudden eddies of cold wind had seemed no more than omens of nightfall until the first rush of rain sent them sprinting under the nearby trees – a stunted lot, struggling in the grip of brambles, but adequate to keep off the weather, for a bit.

Joe lolled gingerly against a scrawny rowan and listened to the leaves take a battering overhead. Emmy found a patch of soft, flaky ground and settled down, her back against a small boulder. Her summer dress and bare arms and legs seemed to give off light in that dim place as she sat absorbed, her face close to the iris leaf she was folding and twisting with such care.

'Didn't you ever make boats out of leaves, Joe?' she asked, taking up the conversation interrupted by the rain.

'Nope,' he said, almost a voice from a tree, a tree with pale bony wrists hooked round its middle.

'I thought everybody did. The older kids used to teach us, oh, all sorts of lore about plants – what you could eat and what you couldn't. I wish I could remember half of it. Didn't you rub dockens on your legs when you got stung by nettles?'

'You know me – can't tell a dock from a dandelion. Nettles, yes – you've seen our garden – but that's as far as it goes. Did you notice the ones we just passed? Never seen such monsters!'

'Mm. Huge.'

'Some nutter must be cultivating them. Maybe it gets you that way, if you stay here too long.'

'Nettles thrive in ruins. That was somebody's home, not so long ago. I suppose this was the end of the garden.' She picked up a pallid fuchsia blossom and tucked it over one ear. It fluttered to the ground as soon as she bent over the leaf again. 'The hedge has all grown wild. It's sad, isn't it? Did you hear them on the boat, saying there used to be more than five hundred people living here? Now there's only a few families.'

His attention had drifted. He spotted a likely branch and tried to chin himself on it. With a dull wrenching noise the branch gave way, and the surrounding trees retaliated with a shower of rainwater.

She let the iris leaf drop. 'Vandal, Joe.'

'What a place!' He peered defensively through bouncing foliage. 'Nothing but ruins and dry rot.'

'You're certainly not making it dryer.'

'It's haunted, too.' He dragged the neck of his tee shirt up to his eyes and haunted her.

'Oh, give over!' she said, laughing at his scarecrow antics.

'Anything you say.' He tugged the shirt back into place. 'Come on, it's getting worse. Let's run for it back to the hotel.'

They argued confusedly over the distance involved.

'It's too far to make a run for it. We took ages, coming,' Emmy insisted.

'Ah, but you forget how long you spent chucking stones in the sea and petting those moth-eaten cows.'

'We still came quite a way. Think how much the shape

of Sheep Island has changed since we started out from the hotel.'

'Sheep Island? Where did you hear about Sheep Island? We only got here this afternoon!'

'I know because I asked. That nearest little island is called Sheep Island because they used to take sheep across at low tide to graze there. What's the time, anyway?'

'After ten.' He peered at his wrist-watch. 'It's too dark to see a bloody thing . . .' He fished in his trouser pocket and brought out a bunch of keys with a tiny flashlight attached. A cone of yellow light perched briefly over the watch face. 'Twenty-five past.'

She watched him tuck the gadget away. 'Neat, that . . . How d'you like my boat?' She held it up, sighting along it and tweaking her handiwork into trim – a narrow skiff with its bow curled up and over in a circle. 'That's the sail, believe it or not. We could go and float it in the sea, if it wasn't pouring.'

'If you're ready, let's make tracks, love. This rain means business, in spite of the forecast.'

He held out a hand and pulled her upright, kissing her until she had found her balance. 'Love me, Emmy?' he whispered in her ear as they clung together.

'Love you, Joe. Love you so it hurts.'

'Have to get you back, though, sweetheart. That thin dress – '

'I'm all right, really I am. Oh this rain's too bad! Imagine, Joe – just when we needn't watch the clock for my folks coming home.'

'Do you think I can stop imagining – but just listen to it! What a downpour!'

Indeed the trees no longer had any shelter to give, sending down chilly jets that soaked more thoroughly than rain. With great reluctance they separated and began to ease through tangled branches, holding them back for each other.

'It smells so good,' Emmy said after a while. 'Know something? The people opposite us are going to put concrete over their front garden.'

'I expect they need it to park their car.'

'As if we hadn't enough rotten concrete to look at! I wish I could take some of this back. The smell of it, even. A weekend's far too short. In the town you forget how real trees and things smell in the rain.'

'Foisty,' said Joe, thrusting ahead.

She caught up with him, tugging his hand. 'This'll all smell different when the sun's out tomorrow. We used to – '

'Oh, drop it, Emmy! OK, you had great times in the Hebrides when you were a kid on holiday. I came here to please you – anywhere so I could be with you. And what do I get? A guided tour of every damn cowpat!'

'But I only want to . . .' Her voice gave out. When it revived a bit, she said, with a catch in her throat: 'I talk too much. I know it. Point taken.'

They pressed through the barbed, flailing darkness. Lightning flared, leaving a tracery of twigs and leaves dazzling their eyes. They froze instinctively as thunder thickened the dull roars of the firth.

'We seem to be walking into a cliff,' Joe said. 'Did you see?'

'Yes.' She giggled. 'We've come the wrong way.'

'Well then, about turn.'

'No, wait!' she cried, excited, holding him back. 'Listen! I can hear water!'

That made him shout with laughter. She felt his ribs quivering under the damp cotton, and jerked her hand away.

'No – ' She was angry. 'Not the rain. Not the sea. There's a waterfall, I'm sure there is!'

She tossed the wilting iris leaf at him and ducked away among the trees. In a few seconds she was free of them and up to the knees in thick wet grass, her feet sucked at by bog. Slithering and tripping in the dark, she stumbled against one of the rough boulders that lay half-buried in the grass, falling heavily across it.

Joe caught up with her. 'What the hell was that for?' he demanded, lifting her none too gently by the shoulders. 'You deserve to break your neck!'

'Let go, I'm all right.' She maintained her dignity somehow, rubbing a grazed shin.

'What got into you, barging off like that?'

'I didn't want you to stop me getting to the waterfall.'

' – Madness. Come on, let's get out of this bloody wilderness. You can't hunt waterfalls at this time of night.'

'Too late – I've found it! You can just make it out, over there – ' she pointed. 'I'm sure there's a cave too, and we can dry out – '

The idea had some appeal. 'But what makes you think there's a cave?'

'They were talking about it in the bar.'

'They were talking about one on the mainland.'

'But I heard them! They said it was opposite Sheep Island!'

'Christ, not again! I don't know where you get all this – they were talking about a big cave the tinkers use, on the mainland. Come on, it's daft hanging about here.'

She leaned forward and cupped his cheeks between her hands. 'Come and look at the waterfall. It's such a little one, all to ourselves. The rain's going off a bit. Please.'

'Well . . . I suppose we can't get much wetter. Let me go ahead, though. I don't want you disappearing down a pot-hole in the dark. You've scared me enough for one night.' He led the way, trailing her by the hand. 'If it gets any boggier we're turning back.'

The ground dipped, seemed to settle in morass, then rose quickly and steeply till it became a kind of boulder-strewn beach under the overhang of the cliff. They were walking along the bottom ledge of the rock that towered into stormy darkness overhead. To one side, the waterfall tumbled in thin streamers.

There was no daylight to favour sight, and darkness gave room to the other senses. The enormous arch of cliff weighted their ears with stillness and the swiftly falling water patterned the night with sound. Their hands reached into the water and came spilling back for their mouths to taste. Then they drank thirstily, and slid arms round one another's warm, slender waists, pressing faces side by side where the skin still burned from the day's salt and sun.

A glimmer or two in the clouds lit up the flying drops and revealed the abundance of ferns and grasses that festooned the place. Every crack, every fissure in the old rock, every cranny where a seed could lodge or a root find hold was burdened with lush greenery, and the wind stirred in it, hissing and shaking free the smell of loam and moss.

Joe brought out the flashlight and played it around. A frog surprised them, goggling up into the light with a sick grin, his throat working like a bellows. When they had admired him enough, Joe turned the light aside and let the small, damp shadow flop stoically on its way. They began to follow the yellow plaque of light along the drenched rockface, past balustrades crowned with fern and tilting slabs slashed with ore, past faults and flaws so deep the whole edifice might topple, and buttresses so broad they would withstand forever.

Rounding one of these, they found a hollow where two great towers of rock leaned together. Hardly a cave, certainly not one that could house a tinker family, this shadowy lean-to with walls bulging down at an angle into the packed earth. A basement attic, they called it, testing the soundness of its bulges. A place to make love, they conspired, not believing their luck. Even here, minute hanging gardens struggled in the dry cracks. The light floated like a bubble and settled on one of them. Joe plucked a green thing no bigger than his fingernail and laid it on Emmy's palm, the torch close over it.

'It's perfect – a miniature violin! You wouldn't think it could be that small,' she whispered, and caught a glimpse of his proprietorial grin.

He turned the light back to the worn rock. 'Odd,' he muttered. The light wavered on one spot.

Emmy came and peered over his shoulder. 'What is it?' she asked in his ear.

'I'm not sure – a sort of design cut right into the rock.'

She wanted the torch held closer.

'You don't suppose it's been carved?' he wondered, flashing the light about. There was nothing that explained his find. 'Were there cave-men in this part of the world?'

'I've no idea.' She reached over his shoulder and probed tentatively at the deep parallel cuts which tapered off to a point. The cuts were fluted along the edges, the longest no more than three inches. 'It looks as if it's been the tip of a bit of bracken – '

'I think it's meant to be an arrow-head. The rest of the carving must have worn away.'

Emmy pointed out gently that there were no tool marks.

'How would you explain it, then?'

She hesitated. 'It isn't man-made, Joe. It's the imprint of a fern, millions of years old.'

He grumbled disbelief.

'It's a fossil, honestly.' She slipped her arms under his tee shirt and held him tightly. 'Just thinking about it makes me feel weird. I wonder what this place was like then . . . I can't begin to imagine a thousand years even, let alone a million.'

He was moving his fingers slowly over the imprint as if it were a sign in Braille. '. . . Because people haven't got that kind of time.'

'But don't you think, sometimes, we get a look in – for a minute or two – '

Lightning zipped in all directions, hurling jagged shadows. They whirled round and pressed their backs on the rough rock, staring startled into the blinded dark, their arms round each other protectively. Thunder came like hooves pounding along the height of the cliff. They felt it drumming through the rock into their bones and waited for the rock to split like the sky into a maze of splintering cracks. Monstrous, the storm hammered on their shelter, closing them inside a streaming, beaded curtain of hail. Finally it abandoned them there, and began to retreat, growling and slavering, into the distance.

'Oh, Joe,' said Emmy, taking deep breaths. 'Talk about the gods being angry!'

He stroked her hair. 'Not with us, love.'

He spread his tee shirt where their heads could rest and drew her down on to the floor beside him. Quickly she unbuttoned her dress while his hands impatiently pushed the thin material from her shoulders, and they began to make love, lost to all consciousness of their surroundings.

When they drifted back to awareness, it wasn't only the ache of their bodies on the hard floor that roused them. Joe heaved himself to a sitting position, head tilted, listening. Slowly, her eyes barely open, Emmy sat up beside him, snuggling against his back as she handed him his shirt.

Shaking the grit from it, he groaned: 'Am I hearing things?'

'Me too – bagpipes at this time of night!'

'Christ, now I know what that thing in the rock is – a Stone-Age amplifier.'

They hugged and laughed, still bemused with loving, reluctant to let each other dress. They hardly noticed when the piping came to a finish. Eventually they began to put on their clothes. Joe got up and pondered over the leaf shape in the rock. 'I don't know . . .' he said. 'This whole scene's an anachronism.' He turned and stood looking out of the triangular opening, tucking his tee shirt into the waist of his flares. 'God, what a place . . .'

She came pressing beside him, buttoning up her dress. 'What is it?'

A three-quarters moon blazed over the black mainland hills and silvered the placid firth where the islands floated. Across the near shore stretched the frail trelliswork of the woods where they had lost their way. No wind stirred the trees now nor rustled the nearby ferns and grasses. There was no sound at all but the hush of the sea, and the splash of the waterfall somewhere along the shadows of the cliff. One sign of life only, one flickering pinprick of light at the foot of the far hills, near the glistening water, drew their eyes.

'A campfire?' Emmy wondered.

More than once it went out for a few seconds, then glittered as before.

'Somebody's crossing in front of it,' Joe guessed. 'That must be where the big cave is.'

A dog barked hoarsely, so far away that their senses

strained after the sound. Then the pipes began again. A single high, held note unravelled into a slow lilting tune. The moon slid higher, drifting in and out of trails of smoky cloud. The spark of fire vanished and lit, and vanished and lit, and the pipes cried thinly across the water, refined beyond belief.

They listened to the end, as if to a story. When the last long-drawn echo had faded out of hearing, the point of light ceased to blink, shining out again, clear as a star. At length the cool of night touched them, and they shivered and began to move, surprised to find their fingers so cramped with holding that, unlocked, they were as crooked as dry twigs.

Slowly they took a last look all round. Joe cleared his throat: 'Ready?' He jingled the keys with the clever flashlight attached. Pointing it across the firth, he signalled a rigmarole of dots and dashes.

'What's all that about?' Emmy wanted to know.

'It means: "Please reserve cave for two, August Bank Holiday."'

'Three nights on a hard floor?'

'A sleeping bag, a Primus stove, and thou – '

'Joe, sweetheart, we've still to find the road back.'

'He isn't replying. Maybe he's booked up.'

Joe reached for her hand and tucked it with his own into his trouser pocket. They wandered down the moonlit grassy slope, and as they went, the far hills leaned lower on the horizon, preparing for another million years.

BIOGRAPHICAL NOTES

JANET CAIRD was born in Nyasaland (now Malawi), and educated at Dollar Academy and Edinburgh University. After graduation she studied at the Sorbonne and Grenoble University. She is married to James B. Caird, District Inspector of Schools for Ross and Cromarty, and lives in Inverness. She has published one children's book, *Angus the Tartan Partan*, and five novels, *Murder Reflected*, *Perturbing Spirit*, *Murder Scholastic*, *The Loch*, and *Murder Remote*.

ROBERT A. CRAMPSEY was born in Glasgow in 1930. M.A. (Hons) History, 1951, A.R.C.M., 1958, Brain of Britain (BBC) 1965, Churchill Fellow (USA) 1970. Author of *The Game for the Game's Sake* (History of Queen's Park Football Club) 1967, *Puerto Rico* (David and Charles Islands series) 1972, and *Guadeloupe* (forthcoming in the same series). Radio and TV broadcaster and playwright. Presently Rector of St Ambrose High School, Coatbridge.

KIRKPATRICK DOBIE was born in 1908. Retired Grain Merchant. Educated Loreburn Street School, Dumfries, and Dumfries Academy. Literary work (confined to Writers' Workshop, Dumfries, an Extra-Mural class of Glasgow University) includes poems published with others as *A Fatal Tree*, 1971.

GILES GORDON was born in Edinburgh in 1940, and brought up there. He now lives in London with his book illustrator wife and three children. His most recent publications are *Farewell, Fond Dreams*, a collection of his stories, and – as editor – *Prevailing Spirits*: a book of Scottish ghost stories. Last year he was C. Day Lewis fellow in writing at King's College, University of London.

WILLIAM GRANT was born in Glasgow. Father docker. Miseducated Glasgow. Misqualified for secondary school; spent three years sawing pieces of wood. Joined Merchant Navy, ejected from Merchant Navy. Joined Royal Navy, ejected from Royal Navy. Then briefly – bus conductor, truck driver, hospital porter, railwayman, cleansing dept., plastics finisher. Finally entered harbour as docker. Decided, while grafting in the belly of a hold, that if he learned to write he'd earn a fortune. Is at present researching to find out if madness is in any way inherent in the Grant Clan.

P. M. HUBBARD was born in 1910 and now lives in Galloway. Three of his four grandparents were Scottish. His staple ouput is suspense novels, but he also writes short stories, verse and non-fictional prose.

ALAN JACKSON was born and brought up in Edinburgh. His poetry has been published in many literary magazines and he has published two collections – *The Grim Wayfarer* (Fulcrum) and *Idiots are Freelance* (Rainbow Press). He is well-known for the many public appearances he has made on the poetry reading circuits in Britain. A selection of his work appeared in *Penguin Modern Poets 12*.

CARL MACDOUGALL was born in Glasgow and now lives in Fife. Published two story collections, *A Cuckoo's Nest* and *A Scent of Water* (both Molendinar Press, Glasgow) and has had poetry and prose work published in a number of Scottish magazines. He has worked extensively with children in creative writing projects through the Scottish Arts Council's Writers in Schools scheme and has written folk songs, of which the most famous is probably *Cod Liver Oil and Orange Juice*. Presently writing a novel.

GORDON MCGILL was born in Glasgow in 1943, entered journalism in Aberdeen and moved to Fleet Street with the *Sunday Mirror*. After two years in New York working primarily for the *Daily Mail* he is currently freelancing in London. He has written one novel – *Arthur* – which won a Scottish Arts Council award in 1975.

BIOGRAPHICAL NOTES

GEORGE MACKAY BROWN was born in Stromness, Orkney, and has lived there all his life apart from a few student years in Edinburgh. He began by writing verse but has recently moved more and more to prose. His second novel, *Magnus*, was published in 1973, and a new volume of short stories in 1974.

PAUL MILLS was born in Cheshire in 1948. In 1966 he went to Edinburgh University and has lived in Edinburgh until recently. He was given a Gregory Award in 1970 and his first book of poems *North Carriageway* was published by Carcanet Press in February 1976. Other work has appeared in Lines Review, Poetry Nation, Trio: *New Poets from Edinburgh*, and *Made in Scotland*, also published by Carcanet, and has been broadcast on Radio 3. 'Bread' is his first short story.

NAOMI MITCHISON was born in Edinburgh and now lives in Kintyre. Was for many years a member of Argyll County Council and started their travelling art collection for schools. As member of the Highland Advisory Panel got to know most of the Highlands.

GRAHAM PETRIE is 36 years old, born in Malaya of Scottish parents, educated at Dollar Academy, St Andrews, and Brasenose College, Oxford. He moved to Canada in 1964 and has taught at McMaster University, Hamilton, Ontario since then. He has published several short stories, film criticism in several magazines and a book, *The Cinema of François Truffaut*.

ANNE TURNER was born in Glasgow and educated at Whitehill School; now lives in Leeds where she works as a secretary. Her work has appeared in many periodicals and has been anthologized and broadcast.

OSWALD WYND was born in Tokyo and lived in Japan until he was nineteen, then went to the U.S.A. Emigrated to Scotland in the thirties, where he has remained ever since, except for war service in the Far East and three and a half years as a Japanese POW. He has written fourteen novels as Oswald Wynd, and ten as Gavin Black. Lives in Crail, Fife.

ARTHUR YOUNG is the pen-name of a Scottish family doctor. Educated at Hamilton Academy and Glasgow University. Now practises in a New Town. Lately came to serious writing and encouraged by the fact that his contribution has now been accepted for all four volumes of *Scottish Short Stories*.